ELIXIR

ELIXIR

James O. Sy, PhD

Professor of Chemistry
Pasadena City College

ELM HILL

A Division of
HarperCollins Christian Publishing

www.elmhillbooks.com

Elixir

Published in Nashville, Tennessee, by Elm Hill, an imprint of Thomas Nelson. Elm Hill and Thomas Nelson are registered trademarks of HarperCollins Christian Publishing, Inc.

Elm Hill titles may be purchased in bulk for educational, business, fund-raising, or sales promotional use. For information, please e-mail SpecialMarkets@ ThomasNelson.com.

Publisher's Note: This novel is a work of fiction. Names, characters, places, and incidents are either products of the author's imagination or used fictitiously. All characters are fictional, and any similarity to people living or dead is purely coincidental.

Scripture quotations marked NKJV are from the New King James Version*. © 1982 by Thomas Nelson. Used by permission. All rights reserved.

Scripture quotations marked WNT are from the Weymouth New Testament. Public domain.

Library of Congress Cataloging-in-Publication Data

Library of Congress Control Number: 2018947608

ISBN 978-1-595558176 (Paperback)
ISBN 978-1-595557698 (Hardbound)
ISBN 978-1-595557971 (eBook)

This is a thrilling, highly entertaining science fiction novel. It is the first installment of a six-part sci-fi series.

Book One slowly unfolds the events that lead a college sophomore to discover the powers he possesses, powers that are not of this Earth. This first installment is replete with religious themes and teachings. It also narrates the protagonist's first encounter with an extraterrestrial being, and how he stumbles upon a miracle cure—an elixir.

The protagonist's father and missionary grandparents are used by the author to express his personal religious beliefs and convictions.

Contents

CHAPTER 1

SWEET BABY JAKE

The phone started blaring: "...*Just the way you are...*"

JT groggily reached out and tried to hit the snooze button, but his clumsy attempt to do so failed miserably. He knocked the phone down to the floor instead. The shattering of the glass cover of his phone simultaneously forced him to instantly wake up from a dazed stupor and caused him to let out a loud and annoyed yelp. "Darn it!"

He knew all too well that his mom, who had grudgingly paid $120 to replace the damaged window glass of his iPhone 8 just last week, would go ballistic with him. His relationship with his mom wasn't all that smooth. Ever since his parents separated and his dad moved away, his mom centered her affection and focus on him. It was nice sometimes, but most of the time, he felt irritated by her overprotective and mother hen treatment of him.

He felt so suffocated that when he was given the choice to decide which school to enroll in, UC (University of California) Irvine or UC San Diego, it was a no-brainer to choose UCSD for his premed biology study. San Diego is two hours away from Glendale, where his mom lived, while Irvine is a shorter ride.

He felt that the distance was good enough of a physical barrier from the frequent, though well-intentioned, badgering of his mom.

Yet sometimes a monkey wrench gets thrown in, even in the best of plans. Mary, Jake's mom, is a hospital nurse who worked on weekends. But because she missed her only son, she changed her work schedule so she could do the weekly weekend drive to San Diego to visit him.

Well, JT (as Jake's dad fondly called him) knew deep in his heart that it was just his mom's way of showing her care, her love, and her affection for him. But he got terribly embarrassed whenever his mom showed up for her weekly visit. Oh, he relished the delicious home-cooked meals that his mom would bring, but he got terribly mortified whenever Mary showed up at the apartment he shared with several other roommates. They started calling him "Sweet baby Jake" or "Sweetie." He is two years younger than most of his roommates, having been academically accelerated by two grades by the principal of his high school. This was after his homeroom teacher found out that his bored and lackadaisical attitude was due to his having already learned the subject matter.

That was the advantage of having his dad living with them then, during his early formative years. His dad, Jerry, had a doctorate in biochemistry. He wanted Jake to excel in math and the sciences, just like him. So the young JT was forced to study and got tutored two hours every day.

The fact that he is two years younger than his roommates, coupled with his mom's uninhibited, outward display of affections for her only son in front of his roommates, led to even more mockery and frequent derision. Trying to escape from all this mean-spirited taunting, he started hiding in the library on days when his mother would come over to visit. This deliberate avoidance—on top of the tedium of the long, four-hour round-trip drive between Glendale and San Diego—made Mary quit her weekly trips.

JT is two weeks away from the end of his second year at the university. It had not been an easy transition for him. He had been coasting along every step of the way in high school, exerting minimal effort and yet getting excellent grades—mainly due to his uncanny eidetic memory and not-too-normal ability to put in an all-nighter in terms of last-minute studying. His dad, although they only kept in contact occasionally, was quite upset by his bad habit of perpetual procrastinating. Jerry jokingly told him, "JT, if they award medals for being the supreme procrastinator, you will, hands down, be awarded the gold medal. You are the world's number one expert on dillydallying, an unparalleled procrastinator."

While trying very hard to shake off his still-drowsy and sedated-like condition, he slowly and droopily forced himself out of bed, fully aware that a quick jolt of energy was needed in order for him to turbo charge everything, if he wanted to have even an iota of a chance to arrive on time for his chemistry class. This wasn't always the case. But his health had taken a nasty and infuriating turn for the worse ever since he suffered from a near-fatal bout of pneumonia, compounded by a severe case of bronchitis. That dreadful episode left him almost at death's door. It had put him in a state of periodically lethargic and weakened condition, and it was recurring in increasing frequency lately.

However, he kept it to himself. For he knew quite well that sharing this information about his physical condition with his beloved mom would only trigger and bring forth her mother hen behavior. Dealing with her over-the-top doting wasn't something he needed right now.

Although a great many of the UC professors didn't mind an occasional tardiness, his asinine chemistry instructor salivated over the prospect of occasionally berating students who had the temerity of coming late to class.

Not wanting to be one of the poor souls who got subjected to a very unpleasant and very public tongue-lashing, he drew from his inner reserve of strength the requisite willpower to spring into an incredible, break-neck efficiency. He hurriedly washed his face with ice-cold water, trying to shake off any residual lethargic feeling from last night's restless and fitful sleep. He didn't even bother to brush or floss his teeth; rather, he took in a mouthful of Listerine, forcibly gargling away, in an effort to erase any vestiges of morning bad breath, while quickly exiting out of his apartment with his skateboard tucked under his left arm. He hastily hopped onto his skateboard and expertly navigated his way around a confusing multitude of students, who were trying to get to their own classes.

Just when he thought he was fortunate enough to get to his chemistry class on time, tragedy struck. He was blindsided by a novice skateboarder who sped with such reckless abandon, so much so that the collision occurred without even giving JT a millisecond of a chance to try to maneuver away to avoid the crash. The impact knocked him off his skateboard, hurling his board like a rudderless missile and disintegrating it upon impact with the side of the building.

While not initially noticing the large gash running along a portion of his lower left leg, he muttered angrily while picking up the remnants of his obliterated skateboard, "No more 'made in China' stuff for me."

CHAPTER 2

An Unnatural
Superpower?

Finally, as he became aware of the large gash on his left leg, JT froze into a panic. Not because of the copious amount of blood steadily dripping from his lacerated flesh, nor due to anticipation of the much -needed but excruciatingly painful process of stitching up the tear, but rather, what really terrified him was the vivid mental picture of his mom's reaction upon getting notified of this unfortunate incident.

He could visualize his mom quickly leaving the nurses' station, only informing a coworker about his mishap but not even bothering to seek permission from her supervisor. He knew how many times his mom had gotten into big trouble and had been severely reprimanded for not follow-ing the standard procedure for these types of situations.

There were three instances that he could distinctly recall where Mary was warned about being pink-slipped because of her poor judgement or ill logic of hurriedly rushing over to be at her only son's side whenever incidents, big or small, happened to her "baby" Jake. He considered her mom fortuitous in a way. But in reality, it was more due to the fact that all of her coworkers, supervisors, and patients loved the excellent care she provided, as well as her no-nonsense dedication to her craft, that she wasn't terminated on the spot. Her bosses begrudgingly turned a blind eye to these instances of insubordination, for they grimaced at the alternative: spending copious amounts of time and utilizing oodles of precious resources training a greenhorn nurse to be his mom's replacement.

So, he hastily took out his handkerchief and used it to wrap around the wound to stop the flow of that vital, shiny red fluid. He politely waved off gracious offers of help from the now growing number of curious students gathered around him, choosing instead to gingerly walk to the health clinic unassisted.

Upon reaching the clinic, he begged, coaxed, and cajoled Joan, a health clinic nurse, not to call or text his mom about the accident. Joan relented, familiar with Mary's over-the-top tendencies in these types of situations. Springing to action, Joan gently cleaned the wound, injected some anesthetic, then delicately stitched up the tear, applied a smidgen of Neosporin, and finally used a sterile gauze and some tape to bandage the wound.

Jake, exhausted by the whole ordeal and already very late to class, decided to instead hobble his way to his place and just rest up. He spent a great amount of energy to half-drag and half-hobble his weakened body across the campus to get to his apartment. Even though the poorly-maintained place was but a stone's throw away from the university, it still required Herculean effort on his part just to reach it. He attributed this to the lingering effects of the medical malady that he suffered almost three years ago, also to the fact that he had skipped his breakfast and the rawness of his newly stitched wound. It was a very painful task; he reacted by alternately shouting, screaming, cursing, and gritting his teeth throughout, since the numbing effects of the local anesthesia had started to wear off. He now felt sharp, intense pain from the wound, compounded by the soreness of his stiches. He was even in a much pitiful circumstance when he reached the elevator on the ground floor of his apartment. He stared incredulously at the crude, handwritten sign posted on one of the doors of the rickety elevator: OUT OF ORDER.

This string of unfortunate turn of events catapulted him to losing it.

Using the only usable scrawny right leg, he took out his frustrations by kicking with such brute force the pair of newly installed elevator doors (the old ones were rusty). Much to his shock and horror, the kick turned those doors into a crumbled pile of twisted, useless pieces of metal.

"What the hell?" he blurted out, stunned.

CHAPTER 3

THE DISTANT DAD

This chapter is heavy on things related to the purpose of human existence.

Not wanting to get into a deeper heap of trouble, and trying hard not to attract any unwanted attention, he did his best to escape from the "crime scene" by doing a combination of semi-hopping and soft, tiptoeing motion.

Once he reached the foot of the stairs that led to his unit upstairs, he let out a deep sigh of relief. He began the long, arduous climb to his apartment on the third floor, doing it nonchalantly at first, but increasing his pace after he reached the second floor. He imagined that the door of his unit on the third floor beckoning him welcomingly, offering refuge from the unexplainable demolition he just performed on those brand-new elevator doors.

He isn't a bad kid, knowing there isn't a chance in hell that he would escape the responsibility, or even not owning up to the incident. Having learned from his dad's strict, upright, God-fearing indoctrination of him, he realized that what he just did is tantamount to willful desecration. Although his relationship with his dad isn't strained, it is, at best, cordial and distant.

Oh, he worshipped his dad. He knew that his old man is very

intelligent, and a good person. Jerry has God-given talents, and an ability to express ideas and concepts into words and mental pictures that were easy to grasp. Jerry spent time as a college professor. He had the knack and the uncommon ability to teach and explain difficult and complex topics, making use of illustrations, analogies, and funny jokes to transform mind-taxing, thought-provoking abstract theories into something that students could easily comprehend.

His former students loved him because he created a very relaxed, inviting, entertaining, and conducive learning environment. He was an excellent wordsmith: weaving, polishing, and hammering words into poetry and vivid mental images. He possessed the skillfulness of a stand-up comedian, transforming the boringness of a one-hour-and-a-half-long typical chemistry lecture into a highly entertaining, humorous, and laughter-filled learning experience. His classes were always oversubscribed, and it always irritated him that he couldn't accommodate more students into his extremely popular, always-in-demand courses.

What got him into trouble sometimes was when he, on occasion, got offtrack while lecturing. It is in moments like these that landed him in hot water, because he was different in his thoughts and beliefs than ninety-nine percent of the people.

Take, for example, his spin on the common perception of Hell and Heaven. Many religions advocate the idea that Heaven is a place where good, God-fearing, Christ-centric people go after their temporal stay here on Earth ends, while Hell is a place reserved for bad people: the murderers, the rapists, the fake prophets and charlatans, the sexual predators/abusers, etc. But Jerry adhered to the idea that Heaven and Hell have more to do with existence vis-a-vis that of a supreme, Omnipotent Being (in the case of Christians, that powerful being is called God). Hell is existence without or away from God, while Heaven is when you are in harmony or having a God-centric existence. So, in this context, it is very possible that some people are already experiencing a Heaven-on-Earth type of existence.

JT's relationship with his dad became distant, not due to the fact that Jerry moved away after he separated from Mary; not because of his mom's constant attempts of putdowns or the highlighting of his father's perceived shortcomings (related to her insecurities about losing out of Jake's love and affection), either. It was definitely because Jerry was trying to tailor his young son's life into something bordering on madness.

Jerry believed that every human is but a slave chained to financial bondage. We work long and hard hours just to earn money to meet our daily needs and sustenance. But because of the constant efforts, grind, struggles, and much energy expended to eke out a daily living, humans lose sight of their true purpose. And for those who are enlightened, they are mostly unwilling or unable to heed our noble calling because of financial predicament. For it would take a semblance of financial independence—without any worry about earning money to pay for food, shelter, gas, children's tuition, medicine, and the like—for each one of us to get unshackled.

Once free, we could fully and wholeheartedly commit to our noble and true calling: That we came into existence in this physical world to make it a better place.

We are not born into this world to be consumers and exploiters of Earth's finite resources; rather, we are to become warriors. A group of hardworking, dedicated foot soldiers tasked to be used as instruments, as deliverers of God's unconditional love, overflowing and bountiful blessings, limitless grace, inexhaustible compassion, and grandiose magnanimity. In and through these committed workers, the unearned grace and benevolent blessings freely given by the Almighty are to be manifested.

It was for this reason why Jake ran, literally and figuratively, from his weird, possibly asylum-bound dad. No way would he want to be a foot soldier.

It truly infuriated his dad even more when, after Jerry's three-hour, one-on-one long proselytizing, JT sarcastically asked, "Can I be a five-star general instead?"

CHAPTER 4

Surprise Waiting at the Door

A few steps from his apartment, JT suddenly started to feel an over-whelming dizziness. Much to his astonishment, he sensed that he was being untethered from the pull of gravity, allowing him to float thirteen inches above the floor. Not only that, he could see the walls starting to buckle and all the objects in his line of sight beginning to swirl around him—slowly at first, then increasing at a sickening pace.

He had a very hazy recollection of events after that, but he distinctly remembered seeing a younger version of himself strapped to a 2.5 feet × 7 feet stainless steel table with strange, menacing humanoids intently looking down at him.

He must have blacked out after that, because a blank mental picture was what he kept getting no matter how hard he tried to recall. When he came to, he found himself sprawled face down on the old and stinky carpet of his room, his face partially caked with a semi-solid, slimy material that was rose gold in color. He could only surmise that this odious, foul-smelling slime must have drooled out from his mouth while he was knocked out, or that he had vomited the nasty stuff.

Much to his chagrin, the disgusting, gooey slime also soiled the pricey Lacoste shirt that his mother had recently gifted him. He hurriedly got up, intent on trying to wash off all the potentially noxious stuff that was stubbornly clinging and sullying his favorite polo.

But no matter how focused and doggedly determined his efforts were of ridding his shirt of the stains, they proved futile. He now felt totally overwhelmed by this growing stack of hapless occurrences: the broken window glass of his smart phone; missing his chemistry class (as a consequence, an extra chore of having to find a classmate to borrow notes of the missed lecture); the unfortunate collision with that inexperienced, careless skateboarder; the still-throbbing, painful cut on his left leg; the arduous (and most probably pointless) chore of removing the stains off the carpet; the possibility of having to get rid of his favorite shirt; and the unpleasantness of going to the apartment manager to own up to and apologize for the damage he did on the elevator doors.

And he still had to think of ways to conjure up the money to pay for the destroyed elevator doors, not to mention the unpleasant necessity of having to confess to his mom if he couldn't secure the funds to pay up by himself. These thoughts went on and on in his mind.

Just when Jake thought things couldn't possibly get any worse, a "… *Jingle bells, jingle bells…*" bit from a familiar Christmas song started playing from the Honeywell musical door chime. He painstakingly forced his very tired and aching body out of the couch. With a cautious dose of trepidation, he delicately limped to the door. His sixth sense, foreboding an impending doom, proved him right.

There, through the peephole, he saw to his horror, his mommy dearest, patiently waiting to be let in. The only thought that crossed his mind as he debated whether to hide under his bed or to pretend that nobody was home was, *I'm DEAD.*

Sardonically, a follow-up thought registered, *Ask for cremation, not burial.*

CHAPTER 5

THE DOTING MOTHER, MARY

With visions of a terrified man, a rope tied around his neck, and helplessly awaiting his execution (although he would have preferred the swift, precise cut of a guillotine), JT resignedly unbolted the door chain and opened the door. His mother briskly walked past him and went straight to the lounge room. He meekly followed, warily settling his bone-tired, pain-racked body into his favorite beige-colored leather chair.

With mouth wide agape and a very worried, shocked expression registering on her blemish-free, porcelain-smooth exquisite face, Mary tried to speak, but all that came out were guttural, indecipherable sounds. The heart-breaking and pitiful image of her "baby" caused her to simultaneously bursts into tears and emit howls of deep despair. But being the profusely loving "mother hen" that she is, Mary immediately snapped out of her appalled state.

First, she helped JT out of his favorite, irreversibly stained Lacoste shirt. Then, she hurriedly went to the drawer to get a clean T-shirt and a washcloth, moistening the cloth with warm water. She gently and soothingly wiped his face, her deep love for him manifested by the tender touch in which she meticulously cleaned his face.

Jake trembled in helpless anxiety, for he knew the unpleasantness of the next thing his mom would do. Her handsome "bambino" (JT would forever be her "bundle of joy," possibly even when he got to be in his forties) was ticklish. Touch his neck area, feet, lower part of both ribs, or his underarms, and he would break into uncontrollable bouts of laughter.

It was funny when he was a young boy. His grandma loved the way he burst into hysterical yet joyful fits of giggling whenever she tickled the soles of his feet. But he found it extremely annoying nowadays when someone tried to tickle him. He even quarreled with his BFF (best female friend) when she sneakily approached him from behind to tickle him.

Even though his mother is now approaching forty-three, her delicate and fine, exquisite features are still evident. Her face seemed untouched by the inescapable ravages of aging. Her delicate countenance is as smooth as the finest china porcelain, unblemished and nary any evidence of crow's feet. The silky smoothness of her elegantly radiant skin gave it a soft tenderness and suppleness. Her face and skin could be a walking advertisement for a cosmetic company (move aside, Cindy Crawford!). And the wonder of it all is that she hated applying cosmetics on her skin and face. She claimed to suffer allergies whenever she applied make-up.

For the majority of people, the unstoppable forward march of time breaks, stiffens, damages the collagens and the elastin fibers, causing these to lose their elasticity, as a result: wrinkles, crow's feet, and aging lines start to appear around the age of late thirties or early forties.

Worse, the oil glands start decreasing in size, making the skin dry, the unattractive consequence of which is that many end up with broken, damaged, or bruised skin.

But due to a combination of a fortunate quirk of nature, a serendipitous assist from good genes, and an application of several blobs of 100% preservative-free, fresh virgin coconut oil thrice a week, her velvety, age-defying alabaster skin remained amazingly pliant and unwrinkled, which would be more surprising if people knew the complex story of her sad, hard life.

CHAPTER 6

ANCESTRY

Mary's father is an ethnic Chinese who was born in Fujian, a south-eastern coastal province of mainland China. The dispersion of some of these mainland Chinese overseas occurred in two distinct periods and for different political and economic reasons.

The furious pace of the first wave of Chinese migration happened from the early 1840s, tapering to a slower pace at around the 1890s. This movement both had a human trafficking and an economic component to it.

The forced migration of these mostly dirt-poor Chinese was due to the "coolie" (loosely translated to mean laborer) trade. It was at a time when the last dynasty of China, the Qin Empire, was starting to crumble and experiencing the beginning of its end. British and American merchants were using the forced repatriation of Chinese "dogs" (how these poor souls were sometimes referred to then) as a source of cheap labor.

The British businessmen were using these destitute laborers as workers in sugar plantations scattered around their colonies, or to work mining guano (an excrement of seabirds and bats that is a good source of fertilizer since it is rich in nitrogen, potassium, and phosphates) in places like Cuba and Peru. The Americans, on the other hand, got those impoverished

Chinese (mostly from the South China province of Guangdong) to build the first transcontinental railroad.

Another group of Chinese also went overseas, but for economic reasons. The discovery of gold in California in the late 1840s attracted voluntary expatriation of poverty-stricken Chinese looking to escape from famine, natural disasters, overpopulation, land shortages, and the Taiping Rebellion (1850-1864).

The diaspora of some Chinese families during the second wave of overseas migration happened due to political reasons.

The Chinese Civil War (1927-1950) was happening, the forces of Generalissimo Chiang Kai-Shek were battling the Communist forces led by Mao Zedong (devotedly called Chairman Mao by his followers).

The intense pace of this wave reached its peak when the victory of the Communist forces was at hand (1949). Many were fleeing because of personal safety concerns and the strong disdain or aversion of living under a Communist regime. Quite a few of these freedom-loving Chinese, along with the remnants of a defeated Kuomintang army, emigrated to the neighboring island of Taiwan. The rest of these poor souls, unwilling to even entertain the idea of living under a new and more oppressive leadership, fled to Southeast Asian countries like Malaysia, Indonesia, Singapore, the Philippines, and so on.

Mary's father, Vicente Sy (probably a name adopted as a way of assimilating to the new country), was one of those who fled from the newly installed Communist regime. He ended up in Manila, the capital of the Philippines, during the late 1940s. But because of his stubbornness and initial reluctance to uproot himself and move to a foreign country, he waited until the last moment to flee. The sad consequence of his poor planning was that he landed with literally only the clothes on his back and nary a penny in his pocket.

He had a hard time adopting to this new country, since he only knew how to speak Fookien, a Chinese dialect, while the natives spoke Tagalog. Worse, he didn't know anybody; neither did he have any relatives. As a consequence, he barely had food to eat. He considered himself fortunate when, one day, he bumped into a kindly fellow Chinese, who hired him to work as a janitor in the businessman's handicraft factory.

Vicente was thankful for having free lodging, albeit he slept on the floor of the factory, and of being nourished by three square meals daily.

Unfortunately, the handicraft business was in its early nascent phase, and so he was paid intermittently. He was fine with his situation for the first few months, but after eight months, when his financial predicament didn't improve, he decided to take his chance and purchased a one-way ticket to the southern Philippines. As luck would have it, he chanced upon a province-mate from good old China.

The kindly old man need workers in his expanding copra (dried coconut meat from which coconut oil are extracted) business, and was too happy to have a fellow Fujianese (what Chinese people from Fujian are called) working for him. Vicente took the opportunity to showcase his hardworking, efficient, dependable, and trustworthy traits.

The old man was very impressed, and not wanting to lose such a useful and industrious worker, he made Vicente a son-in-law by marrying him off to one of his daughters, Trinidad.

The union between Vicente and Trinidad produced a brood of six girls and one son: Felicia (the eldest, also known as Fely); Reginald (the only male, nicknamed Reggie); Anastasia (the girl who fantasized of becoming an immensely wealthy, philanthropic Asian female equivalent of Donald Trump, fondly called Ana); Maria Lourdes (JT's mom, preferred to be called Mary, but the other sisters kept calling her Lourdes just to irritate her); Sharon (whose goal was to become a caring and compassionate nurse); Melinda (also known as Mely, the fun-loving, free-spirited, no-care-in the-world sister); and Christine (the youngest, whom they called Christy, the sole sibling who caught the religious fervor and dreams of becoming a female pastor).

Life was good for every one of the Sy bunch. Enteng (the term of endearment that Trinidad called her husband) was made a partner in the copra business, and his newly-minted upper-middle-class status accorded him the financial resources to provide for his family, having all of them enjoy the trappings of wealth: most expensive private education, legions of subservient maids, chauffeured rides, lavishly grand birthday parties, and, on special occasions, family trips to Disneyland and the Universal Studios.

But no one ever knows what fate has in store for each of us: was rich and now poor; was poor and now rich; was alive, kicking, and enjoying life to the fullest, now dying in bed; was healthy and now stricken with cancer; the list goes on.

Such is the fickleness of human existence. Here one day and gone the next. The uncertainty and the terminus of this temporal sojourn is only known by the Omniscient Creator. The fleeting time we have in this brief physical incarnation is not ours to own—leased to us not for self-centered, greedy existence, but to hopefully be used for the benefit and greater good of all of humanity.

What happened next completely shattered the idyllic tranquility that the Sy family was enjoying immensely.

CHAPTER 7

GENESIS OF A MOTHER HEN

People react to the loss of a beloved all too differently. An extreme example of undying devotion and refusal to let go, of reaction to the sorrowful loss of a loved one, is narrated in the following two paragraphs. This is only used to illustrate, and has no relevance to the story.

A ninety-five-year old widower, unable to let go and accept the fact that his wife of fifty-five years, had passed away. Without remiss and always oh-so-punctual at precisely 7:00 am, he would rouse himself, meticulously groom himself, put on his Sunday best clothes, and beg his retired daughter to drive him to the immaculate grounds of the Rose Hills cemetery in Whittier. Once driven to the tomb where the remains of his beloved wife lay, he would gently place the very fragrant and pretty bouquet of flowers at the foot of her tombstone. None of those cheap flower arrangements, either. It was an elegant and artistically-arranged medley featuring cream lilies; ruby-red, large-headed roses; purple lisianthus; and ivory, large-headed roses tied together with asparagus fern, steel grass, and eucalyptus, all wrapped and tied with a ribbon.

He would start by greeting his wife lovingly, then mournfully admonishing her for leaving him alone. In his hour-long soliloquy, he would alternately berate his deceased wife for having the audacity to abandon him, alone in this physical world; then revealing his deep longing, his

resultant overpowering feeling of loneliness; and, finally, his eager anticipation of their eventual rendezvous. You would think that the passage
of time would diminish his feeling of grief, or that he would tire of his
visitations. But, NO, this was a daily ritual that had been going for two
and a half years.

It is such an undying love that even death don't have the power to
sever this eternal loving attachment.

....

The utopian state of the Sy clan didn't last long, as heartbreaking tragedy struck.

Trinidad was fastidiously supervising the finishing touches of the
large, spectacular garden being built adjacent to their recently-built opu-
lent mansion, when she slipped on a pool of muddy water. Her head hit
the pile of surplus imported Italian marble lying nearby so hard that the
accident irreparably cracked her skull and left her in a coma.

In spite of the valiant efforts of medical specialists to save her, she
passed away two days later.

Of all the brood, this sad incident affected Mary the most. She took
the death of her dear mama so bad that she became withdrawn, barely
engaging in any conversation, and most of the time, she was in a state
of "physically-there-but-really-somewhere-else." She constantly isolated
herself from her siblings by locking herself in her room.

She missed her mama so badly. She missed the time when she was
blissfully basking in the warm, tender, compassionate, gushing love of
her kind, soft-hearted mother. So when that unfortunate tragedy struck,
Mary was devastated, unable and unwilling to accept the fact that her
beloved mama was gone.

Refusing to even bathe and only taking a few morsels of food during lunch or dinner, she became emaciated. Because of her unkempt,
unwashed, and unsanitary condition, her siblings refused to sit anywhere
near her and started calling her, "Stinko."

Vicente was so distressed that he hired the sternest nanny he could find, and gave instructions to force-feed and bathe the "Stinko" daily.

Fully occupied with his highly successful business and realizing the need for a mother figure for his still-grieving children, Enteng remarried. But his choice of wife was terrible. The half-Chinese secretary he chose wasn't only coldhearted but was also devious and condescending. Her relationship with the brood could be described generously as cordial and heartless. There was no evidence of even an iota of care or feeling of love. Most of her time was spent plotting schemes for self-aggrandizement or for enjoyment of her nouveau riche status. At times, her dealings with the siblings led to heated and acrimonious confrontations.

Mary felt even more isolated and neglected, longingly pining for the fun and tender moments spent with her mama. In her moments of solitude and reflections, she vowed to shower undivided, unconditional, and overflowing affection and love to all offspring she might bear.

CHAPTER 8

MIGRATION TO THE GOOD OLD USA

The forward rhythmic march of time has a smooth, salving quality. Foremost, it allows the memory of a shocking or traumatic event to slowly fade away, but most importantly, the longer the amount of time that elapsed, the lesser the degree of grief and pain that remains. That is encapsulated nicely in the old saying: "Time heals all wounds."

That was how it went with Mary. The seven years that passed since her loving mother died dulled the unpleasant pain. It wasn't completely gone, though. The residue of that grief occasionally manifested itself into spontaneous, loud, and uncontrolled crying, sometimes followed by shrieking howls of despair.

But time did *more* than that. For with each grain of sand gently and steadily trickling down the hourglass of time, simultaneously transpiring in military-like cadence, was a stunning metamorphosis. It was an awe-inspiring work of nature in full display: the reed-thin, awkward, tomboyish teen had slowly blossomed into an exceedingly majestic beauty.

That astounding transformation would have put the masterpiece of Leonardo da Vinci, the "Mona Lisa," to shame.

In addition to having that aesthetically-pleasing and unblemished, porcelain-like angelic face, Mary was also blessed with having statuesque, shapely curves at all the right places, and an ampleness in her well-endowed bosom.

What happened next only confirmed that we are mere actors in that theater called life. Fate acted as the puppeteer and we, as hapless puppets, are mindlessly following the script.

In a cruel twist of fate, it was her ravishing beauty that got her into big trouble. She, unfortunately, lived in a province teeming with ruthless Communist rebels, and the leader of the villainous band was unabashedly *smitten* with her.

In his initial visit, Kumander Karding (his nom de guerre) was very friendly and charming. He fawned over Enteng, constantly showering him with duplicitous flattery. But Enteng already knew what the rebel's true intention was. He had already been repeatedly besieged and harassed by numerous men coming from near and far-flung places, from different social strata and from varied economic levels. He had been incessantly hassled and pestered by these legions of admiring men. For the apple-of-his-eyes, his recently-turned-eighteen Mary, with her fine, exquisite features coupled with a *to-die-for* voluptuous body, had aroused these dirty old men's unsatiated carnal desire.

Enteng was very polite and tried to explain the reasons why he could not give away his favorite daughter in marriage yet.

Karding was very gracious and sympathetic, willingly accepting the rejection of his overtures. In his second trip, Karding tried a different tact. He tried playing to the old man's business predisposition. So, he boldly floated the idea of treating the young girl as a chattel. In his proposed laughable barter, he would give five milking carabaos and twenty egg-laying hens to trade for Mary. In any other setting, Enteng would have burst out laughing at the absurdity of the proposal.

But sensing the seriousness of the manner with which the idiotic scheme was presented, the old man wisely and politely declined. The subsequent visits were more threatening, with threats of bodily harm not only to Enteng himself but also to his entire family. His children and house staff were, without exception, very intimidated and scared.

Enteng tried to seek help from the captain of the nearby police precinct. The chief explained that due to the dual directive of fending off the Commies while, at the same time, trying to maintain peace and order, the resulting severe shortage of manpower prevented him from being able to extend the needed police protection. All he was willing to promise was a biweekly patrol of the family's premises.

Old Vicente left the precinct utterly dejected, pondering on his way home what his next move would be.

Upon reaching his mansion, he encountered a team of men threatening everyone in the household. He hurriedly went to look for Karding, who was at the middle of the dastardly group. He tried to appeal to the rebel head to send away his loathsome band, but Karding stopped him and stonily told him, "Hand over your daughter Mary within twenty-four hours or else I will kill your entire family." After issuing the ultimatum, the group ploddingly left. But before leaving, just for the fun of it, they beat up a couple of male house helps.

Moving in lightning-fast reaction to the threatened extermination of his entire family, he gathered all of his children. He lovingly embraced and kissed each and every one of his terrified offspring, promising to join them in a day or two. He then loaded them up into two reliable, well-maintained Ford vans. He instructed his two Filipino drivers to drive nonstop northbound, only halting when they reach the abode of his close friend, Peter, who owned a sprawling estate in Quezon City, located just northeast of Manila.

After taking care of his business and dictating instructions to a subordinate, he embarked on a trip up north to Peter's place. He thanked his close friend's magnanimity for taking in his children. He confided to his wealthy friend his dire predicament.

Acting on his deep familial feelings and hopefully thwarting the threat of his clan's total annihilation, he made the decision of uprooting his entire family and resettling in Manila. Furthermore, realizing that distance might not be enough of a barrier to the evil guerrilla's unrecip-rocated amorous intent, Enteng reluctantly decided on a gut-wrenching decision.

He decided to send his beloved Mary on a one-way trip to America.

CHAPTER 9

SULLIED ROSE

It is always difficult adjusting in a totally foreign environment. The theory prevalent among behavioral psychologists argues that the personality that eventually emerges (in a developing teen) is shaped by some of these important factors:

1) predisposition from genetic makeup (genotype)
2) guidance and mentoring by the parents during the formative years
3) religious teachings/exposure
4) environmental influences

Mary was raised in a very strict and conservative manner. She wasn't allowed to go outside their mansion without permission. Trips to theaters, shopping places, and amusement parks are always with her siblings and heavily chaperoned. Boys and men bold enough to attempt courtship on any of the Sy sisters are contemptuously shooed away from the well-guarded palatial home.

In addition to being exposed to religious enlightenment at the ultra-exclusive, girls-only St. Mary's Catholic High School, more attempts to inculcate religious doctrines and principles included serious Bible study sessions every Friday night and the regular four-hour long worship and church activities on Sundays.

Private tutors were hired not only to help them with their homework, but expected to give the excitable, energetic bunch lively piano and singing lessons.

But all these positive reinforcements, teachings, religious instructions, and preparations in the formative years were no guarantee to having the potency to offset the corrupting influence of a degenerate environment.

Throw a single seed of a flower into a pile of manure and you can get either of two outcomes:

1) You get a fragrant, dazzling rose that has risen regally from that mound of excrement.
   Or
2) You end up with a sickly, stinky, sullied, and unattractive flower, barely piercing through the odious lump of dung.

It takes a great strength of character and incorruptible moral compass to overcome the effects of a debasing environment.

Sadly, because of the urgent manner with which the young Mary was uprooted, in the hope of prying her away from the clutches of that lustful revolutionary, there wasn't enough time to properly instill these highly desirable traits in her.

She fell in with the wrong crowd. Totally alone and away from the warmth, support, guidance, and comfort of family, she did things she would later regret.

Wishing to gain acceptance from the miscreant gang, she did things that were criminal in nature. Because of her religious upbringing, she initially resisted the advances of the testosterone-laden delinquents. But through a combination of skillful flattery, the showering of cash and lavish gifts, the hollow promises undying love and affection, the incessant pleadings and use of the oft-repeated yet misguided advise of "when in

Rome, do as the Romans do," she eventually gave in to carnal cravings. At the height of this doleful episode, she became promiscuous.

The worse thing was, her stepmother had stopped sending Mary her monthly allowance. With no money to pay for tuition, she quit school and started working as a poorly-paid, overworked waitress in a Vietnamese *pho* restaurant.

It was a pitiable turn of events: an innocent, young, rich princess turned to a hapless and broke waitress. She became the antithesis of the fictional Cinderella.

But just like in that fictional story, a Prince Charming came charging in, trying to rescue the damsel in distress.

Fate is always doing its handiwork as the master puppeteer. In the lifetime of each and every creature, there is always an eclectic mishmash of occurrences. For we, as vulnerable and pathetic marionettes, are being deftly manipulated as players in nature's highly entertaining grand opera that easily trounced even the very best of those Broadway productions:

From idly whiling away as a single sperm or egg in that slimy gene pool…to gaining consciousness as that lovable, cuddly bundle of joy…to experiencing the most fun and carefree existence as a child…to encountering the confusing, complex emotions of a hormone-induced physical transformation…to struggling with the trials, frustrations, and tribulations of life…to questioning and trying to comprehend the purpose of one's very existence…to experiencing excruciating agony of failure or defeat…to enjoying the exhilarating and intoxicating feeling of fleeting success…to delighting and being immensely pleasured by the enrapturing feelings of that unforgettable true love…to becoming aware of the temporal nature of our carnal-based sojourn…to witnessing the irreversible ravages of time.

And so in that cold, rainy night that seemed like eons ago, fate dealt a sympathetic hand to a struggling, crushed, and hopeless soul.

While her fine angelic face and stunning beauty remained breathtakingly seductive, she had endured seven years of hard living. In an advanced First World country like the good old USA, it could be quite unforgiving. If one didn't have an education, especially the technical skills for such highly desirable professions like nurses, doctors, engineers, bitcoin miners, software security (anti-hacking) specialists, and the like, then so sorry, friend, but you are out of luck.

One would invariably be either stuck in menial, low-paying, low-skilled demeaning jobs or be underemployed or unemployed. For more than three scores (started in the early 1970s) now, there was a steady erosion of the middle class base, causing an increase in the growing number of poverty-stricken citizens.

Many economists have attributed this sad plight to the uncompetitiveness of some of this country's manufacturing industries (foreign-based companies have much cheaper labor costs), the consequential wholesale disappearance of previously decent-paying manufacturing jobs (even high school level factory workers used to earn salaries according their middle class status), the outsourcing of some of the low-skilled occupations overseas, the poorly-thought-out or lopsided trade agreements, etc.

In such an ultracompetitive financial landscape, there was no chance for Mary, who was then a twenty-five-year-old college dropout, to advance up the economic ladder.

Lacking any sort of training and hardly equipped with technical skills, Mary reluctantly accepted her financial situation, focusing mainly in the grind and hard struggles to eke out a living. She resignedly went through the hustle and bustle of daily living, solely channeling her efforts on surviving to live another day.

It was raining hard, and Jerry was toiling away inside his cubicle, located at a shared faculty office at the community college where he was employed. He was so busy doing last-minute editing of a chemistry final exam he intended to use the next day that he had lost track of time. He even forgot to eat dinner. He glanced at the wall clock: 9:45 p.m. "Damn," he uttered.

He had heard the growling plea from his empty stomach for nourishment earlier, and ignored it. He is now weakened by the energy-sapping effects of skipping dinner. He knew that he had to rush as soon as possible to the Vietnamese pho restaurant across the college before their 10:00 p.m. closing time if he wanted that reinvigorating and flavorful sustenance.

In his haste, Jerry absentmindedly forgot to grab his raincoat, then he sprinted laboriously across the wet and slippery grounds of the public institution. He arrived at the bustling, still-crowded noodle shop dripping wet, totally aware that he had about a minute to place his take-out order of the steaming hot and nourishing bowl of beef *pho*. Anxiously, he called the attention of an Asian waitress nearby, who was furiously wiping away the laminated top of a recently-vacated table.

Upon hearing his call, she turned around and their eyes locked.

"*...Strangers...in...the...night...*"

CHAPTER 10

UNWEDDED BLISS

This was a no-doubter. You could bet your bottom dollar on it. This had the all the fingerprints of that mischievous little tyke. It was hard to figure out how so much incomprehensible impishness be bottled inside that lovable little devil (or angel?). He was probably pissed off, suffering from a severe case of lactose intolerance. This temporary discomfort probably caused him to shoot his love-inducing miniature arrows indiscriminately.

The cherubic-faced little munchkin had used his arrows to spark an instantaneous love between two complete strangers. An irresistible, overwhelming force swept two totally polar opposites together, imbuing in each, in that singular moment of time, a heart-pounding and magical love.

It was a coalescing of "love-at-first-sight" and "love-you-just-the-way-you-are" moment.

"...I'm ready to take a chance again..."

For how else could anyone explain this awe-inspiring, out-of-blue enchantment, forcibly bringing two dissimilar people together?

"...I can't smile without you..."

Jerry is one of those prodigious talents, getting his PhD when he was only twenty-two years old. He is an extrovert, always singing and entertaining a crowd. He is average looking, charming, sociable, sharp-witted, humorous, and polite. Although fast approaching thirty-seven years of age, he isn't really looking for any serious relationship, nor marriage. While he believed that his special someone is somewhere out there, he isn't inclined to actively go looking her. As far as his marital status is concerned, he preferred to let destiny do its thing and deal him whatever card was in store for him.

He was gifted in his ability to explain difficult concepts of chemistry and biology in a way that students understood. His lectures were never boring, since he sprinkled those with jokes, humor, and spontaneous singing of oldies love songs. His former students looked forward to the last few sessions of every semester, because it was always fun and highly entertaining. Every student was given a chance to sing in front of the class for extra credit points (more points if they emote while singing). Some of these undergraduates went to such extremes, like dressing up like Elvis, Old Blue Eyes, Liberace, or Cyndi Lauper.

His modest salary was more than enough to allow him to live in comfort, because he led a Spartan lifestyle. His only lone stab at self-indulgence was when he bought a new ML-320 Mercedes Benz SUV, some years back.

Jerry liked his German-made car since it was very reliable and rarely broke down. He was a generous and giving person. He did weekly deliveries of fresh fruits, fresh juices, and canned goods to the Pasadena City College food pantry for the benefit of students facing food insecurity issues. So, it was no surprise that when he learned of Mary's sad plight and her grueling daily struggles to survive, he generously offered her the spare room in his apartment, at no charge. He figured the money she saved in rent could allow her some needed breathing room from the excessively usurious interest rates that credit card companies were charging her. This is the very dismal reality that our income-challenged working poor face all too commonly. Their paychecks aren't enough to cover their expenses, so they resort to using high-interest-charging credit cards to bridge the difference. The disheartening consequence is that these mounting credit cards bills would not only be albatrosses, but may turn into the figurative alligators that eventually eat the financially-enslaved folks alive.

Although they had been mutually besotted with each other, and blissfully coexisting and sharing Jerry's apartment, the next phase of their relationship didn't progress until a month later.

The night started innocently. The professor came home dog tired and completely exhausted. It had been a long and grueling day's work for him: attending a departmental meeting and another meeting to brainstorm funding ideas for a proposed temporary shelter (Jerry was passionate for these types of noble and just causes) for PCC students facing housing-related issues. Due to the nonstop yearly increases in house prices and a dearth in supply of housing and apartment units, a growing number of collegians find themselves in varying degrees of homelessness. In addition, Jerry held court during his two-hour-long office hours, patiently answering questions and clarifying some of the topics that confused his biochemistry students.

Finally, his workday mercifully ended when he finished teaching and lecturing to two separate groups of eager college coeds. Mary just got out of the shower, feeling refreshed, cleaned up, recharged, and energized. Jerry let himself in to the apartment, thankful that he survived another arduous and challenging day. When they crossed paths in the living room, this modern-day Juliet, invigorated by the hot shower and smelling so fragrantly, looked compassionately at her fatigued Romeo, his wearied face and slumped posture betraying a day's worth of hard work. She gently grabbed hold of his left hand and gingerly led him to her room, intending to give him a soothing back rub and body massage. It was at moments like these when nature took over—two love-struck people in a private and tender moment.

Magically, some amount of natural body chemicals called pheromones were released in the air. The effects of these airborne pheromones caused the complete obliteration of all the restraints to which they had previously adhered.

The evening turned into a very special and memorable night for the two of them.

CHAPTER 11

THE LONG AND WINDING ROAD TO BECOMING A NURSE

While enjoying the transcendental bliss of finally having found that special someone, Jerry was unable to submit himself whole-heartedly to the warm, beckoning embrace of this euphoric emotion, for gnawing and incessantly tormenting his anguished soul was this seething anger about Mary's demeaning job.

He hated intensely the notion of his inamorata toiling away at that Vietnamese noodle house, coming home bone-tired from the day-long repetitive and backbreaking task of artfully balancing a huge tray of six or seven steaming bowls of hot *pho* noodles. Worse, she had to tactfully deal with irate customers who were either furious about the tur-tle-paced arrival of their chow (which happened during the peak lunch and dinner hours) or that the wrong order of noodles was delivered.

The use of her appealing charm and deft diplomatic skills were always necessary to deal with complaints such as the soup of the noodles were too spicy, or the soup wasn't hot enough, or not tasting like the authentic nutriment sold in their native Vietnam, or simply disliking the quality of the ingredients in their broth. But what drove Jerry batty was the innu-merable frequency of the bold, indecent propositions directed at his lover.

So he came up with what he believed was a workable plan. He waited patiently until his Mary got off work. When she arrived at 9:25 p.m., he seated her in one of the chairs at the dining table and discussed a strategy for getting out of her menial occupation. She initially resisted, objecting to the central theme of his proposed course of action. She cut him off abruptly in midsentence. Being a patient, persuasive, and logical man that he was, Jerry was able, in due course, to bring his darling around and warmed to his idea.

The overall objective was to get Mary into a respectable occupation that paid a decent salary. Because she had a tender, caring, and compassionate nature, studying to become a nurse was the logical choice. So here was the nitty-gritty of the game plan:

1) She needed to work at the *pho* place for another three weeks. It was necessary in order to give the Vietnamese owners sufficient time to find and train her replacement.
2) They had to meet with financial aid counselors to explore the resources available for aiding low-income school dropouts who were trying to get back to school.
3) She needed to get enrolled at Pasadena City College and start taking the prerequisite courses for her intended program of study.
4) She had to be admitted to a nursing program and begin the process of acquiring the knowledge and skills to become a competent nurse.
5) She had to successfully complete the undergraduate nursing program with either a bachelor of science or associate of arts degree.
6) She had to pass the California nursing licensure exam.
7) She had to be employed as a registered nurse.

Jerry, being his usual generous self, volunteered to unconditionally support his amour financially during this whole process. This commitment would, in most probability, deplete the modest savings he had stashed away at the Bank of America: The promised $1,000 monthly allowance, additional money for gas and medicine (not money for food, water, utilities, or shelter, since he had already been shouldering all the financial necessities associated with their sharing the apartment); payment for her health insurance; all the costs associated with her schooling (tuition if no grant/aid was possible, expenses for books, and the like); and many more incidental items that needed to be listed down for this enumeration to be complete.

The strategy looked great on paper; it helped a lot that Mary was very eager and willing to follow the game plan. But she knew that this wasn't going to be easy, since it had been seven long years since she even opened a textbook to read.

And from Jerry's estimation, even if all aspects of the plan were to flawlessly come together, in the best-case scenario, the amount of time required was at least four and a half years. But, in retrospect, the estimation of the time aspect of the plan was way too optimistic.

The road to becoming a licensed nurse ended up needing an additional three years.

Why?

An unforeseen arrival had laid waste to the timetable of the well-laid plan.

CHAPTER 12

AN UNEXPECTED ARRIVAL

L ibido is believed to be either prompted, aroused, restrained, or impelled by various influences, such as biological, psychological, and social factors. In addition, health condition and/or medical circumstance; use of miraculous, libido-enhancing drugs; age of the person; state of personal relationships and lifestyle preferences—all of these, in one way or another, play important roles in shaping the sex drive of a person. In biological terms, it is the sex hormones and the array of neurotransmitters that is working on the nucleus accumbens to stimulate or control the libido in homo sapiens.

Work, family, personal situations, peer pressures, cultural dictums and beliefs, and societal norms are some of the diverse social factors affecting the libido. Psychological interpretation and causality of this drive have been extensively and publicly elucidated.

The eminent Austrian neurologist and founder of psychoanalysis, Sigmund Freud, described libido as that inexplicable energy that is created by survival and sexual instincts. It is part of the id and postulated to be the driving force of all behaviors. Carl Gustav Jung, the scholarly Swiss psychiatrist and founder of analytical psychology, in contrast, put forth a different interpretation of libido. Whereas Freud's definition has a more sexual flavor to it, Jung theorized that libido as that psychic energy that can only be released from the grip of the unconscious by bringing up the corresponding fantasy-images.

During her now-much-regretted phase (from age twenty to twenty-two), her inexplicable actions and bewildering behavior were very atypical of Mary's personality. But these were not due to chemical imbalances or propensities, nor some nonexistent childhood event triggering this uncharacteristic behavior. Rather, it was an act of abject surrender to the hopelessness of her miserable fate.

She was on a foreign soil, so far away from the glowing, caring, warm, and protective hands of her family. Here she was in El Monte, California, alone, helpless, penniless, dispirited, hungry, and besieged with indecent proposals from legions of admirers, as well as countless requests from smitten delinquents. Her earlier days of nonselective prolific debauchery was an utter acquiescence to the wretchedness of her inescapable, heartbreaking predestination.

....

Mary was quite flabbergasted and shocked when, five days after that very special night spent with Jerry, she started feeling the unambiguous symptoms of first trimester pregnancy. Those unmistakable signs were the reactions of her body to the high levels of pregnancy hormones.

Pregnancy hormones include estrogens, progesterone, human placental lactogen (hPL), and human chorionic gonadotropin hormone (hCG). Morning sickness, also called "all-day and all-night sickness," include vomiting; wild mood swings; nausea; fatigue; headaches; constipation; food aversions or food cravings; slight bleeding, cramping; tingly, tender, and swollen breasts; faintness and dizziness; raised basal temperature (oral temperature when you first wake up in the morning); and initial weight loss followed by a fifteen- to thirty-pound increase in weight.

What a wide range of unpleasant maladies that the females of our species have to endure to bask in the ecstasy and thrills of motherhood.

An overworked waitress, Mary was now so conflicted and confused with this unexpected and puzzling development. While she was very thrilled and eagerly looking forward to thoroughly enjoying the roller-coaster ride of motherhood, she worried, rightfully so, that this new developing phase in her life would now put a kink into the well-thought-out plans that Jerry had laid out for her. In addition to needing to fully focus and exert extraneous efforts on the difficult task of being a full-time student (it had been seven long years since she had stepped inside a class-room), she now had to deal with the trials, tribulations, and complexities of raising a child. She was distressed, worried that she might not have that inner strength required to maintain a delicate balance between the enormous task awaiting this older back-to-school student and the unenviable challenges of properly nurturing her future little angel.

But the most troubling aspect of this unexpected occurrence was the impossibility of how this came about.

She had been abstinent for the past three years, ignoring and refusing the sexual overtures of many lewd male patrons of the noodle house. She even amusingly recalled the time around two years ago when she was propositioned by a middle-aged and immaculately dressed lady. Even though she was no longer as fresh, as innocent, and as mesmerizing as when she was eighteen, she was still quite a sight to behold. Having an exquisite face and a vivacious personality helped her mitigate the unattractiveness of being slightly overweight. She could still attract an occasional moth to the flame. A more recent series of blushing recollections centered around her interactions with a kindly wealthy man.

She had to utilize every ounce of her deft diplomatic skills to vigorously but firmly fend off the amorous advances of a lonely and unhappily married older gentleman named Willy. Oh, she was very touched by the displays of affection shown by this smitten grandpa: specially delivered artistically and tastefully arranged bouquets of fragrant, ruby red roses; big boxes of Godiva chocolates; gift cards from such places as Starbucks, Benihana, Ruth's Chris Steakhouse, and Din Tai Fung Dumpling restaurant.

While she was flattered by the unsolicited attention, she was terribly

abashed by Willy's very ostentatious display of his unreciprocated feelings of love. She reached a breaking point when the amusing element
of this incessant material display of affections turned to daily bouts of
ridicule and sarcastic taunting from her coworkers. What ingrates! This
is what she got for sharing the boxes of Godiva chocolates with her fellow
workers.

Wishing to put an end into this increasingly exasperating situation,
she sprang to action the moment Willy walked into the noodle place. She
gently pulled him aside, spoke in a hushed tone, and implored the old gentleman to stop showering her with all those thoughtful presents. Imagine
the flabbergasted reaction she felt when she heard what the genial old
chap told her after hearing her pleading: Willy had decided on his own to
make Mary his mistress.

The gist of the offer: Mary had to quit waitressing as soon as possible. He would give her $1,800 monthly allowance for living expenses.
He would provide her with a fully-furnished and fully-paid apartment
unit, which would serve as their love nest. He promised weekly enjoyment of LA Lakers basketball games or LA Dodgers games or a trip to see
an opera. He also mentioned biannual overseas vacations to places like
Thailand, Japan, South Korea, Singapore, or Switzerland.

What gall!

Mary expressed her shock by saying, in her limited knowledge of
Spanish, "*Señor, tener grande cojones!*" After overcoming this dose of
incredulity, she profusely thanked the affable gent but firmly yet politely
rejected his indecent proposal. As a way of ridding herself of all this
unwanted and pesky attention, she also delicately requested Willy to stop
dropping by to visit her.

. . . .

Initially disbelieving this puzzling development, she rushed to the
neighboring Walgreens to buy a pregnancy kit.

All over-the-counter kits practically work the same way, invariably testing the presence of pregnancy hormones in the urine. The dipstick contains a chemical that detects the presence of human chorionic gonadotropin (hCG), which is produced by the body after embryo implants (attaches) to the walls of the uterus. Its sensitivity for hCG varies, depending on the manufacturer, but generally, in the range of 10 mIU/ml (milli-International Units) to 40 mlU/ml. The more sensitive commercial kits can detect the lower end of the range. Some variations of the testing kit tests for the presence of hyperglycosylated hCG (H-hCG), a pregnancy hormone released right after fertilization, theoretically being detectable even before hCG, thereby indicating pregnancy at an even earlier stage.

....

She carefully held the hCG-detecting stick into the free-flowing stream of her first morning pee, then she laid it gingerly on a flat surface and patiently waited. After six minutes, she checked for the results.

Two red lines.

Unbelieving, she did the test a second time. But much to her astonishment, the second test confirmed it. She was on her long and winding journey to motherhood. Undoubtedly, she would be experiencing its up and downs: joy, sadness, anxiety, sufferings, care, love, and hope. She was already experiencing the early stages of pregnancy. Due to her frequent vomiting and resulting lack of appetite, she had lost seven pounds in just the past few days. But that wasn't what worried her the most. She was very distraught that the love of her life, her heaven-sent, adorable Jerry, would come to the incorrect conclusion that she was back to her old promiscuous ways and was sleeping around once more.

Much to her surprise and gratifying relief, Jerry had not exhibited even an iota of negative reaction. On the contrary, he was overjoyed by this unexpected bit of good news. He was basking and rejoicing in his good fortune: that he would be a first-time dad at age thirty-seven.

To celebrate, Jerry took the soon-to-be mother of his son to a fancy restaurant, stopping to pick up a bottle of Moët & Chandon champagne and a Porto's red velvet cake along the way.

·········

The last five and a half months had not been an easy time for Mary. It was a struggle trying to juggle the responsibilities of being a full-time student and having to deal with the trying and occasionally maddening moments of bearing a child. But for the couple, it was well worth it in the end.

Five months and twenty days after that very special and memorable romantic night, their nine pounds bundle of joy, the adorably cute and lovable little cherub, came rushing out to brighten up their lives.

"Hello, World. Please warmly welcome Jake Timothy S. Kirk!"

CHAPTER 13

THE UNOPENED NOTE

This chapter is the continuation of the interactions between JT and his mother in Chapter 5.

As Jake expected and much to his sheer consternation, his mom started to focus her attention on his damp neck and sticky, sweaty armpits. He was about to protest Mary's intentions vigorously, but he sensed that something was bothering her immensely. It was a stark contrast to her usual giggly, jovial self.

So he bit his tongue and tried his best to suppress the uncontrollable bouts of giggling that invariably followed whenever the sensitive parts of his body got touched. He submitted resignedly while his doting mom, in a series of rhythmic stroking motions, delicately wiped off viscid sweats and some oily deposits from his neck, chest, back, and armpits.

Unable to hold back any longer, he asked, "What's wrong, Mama?"

She tried to open her mouth to answer, but no words came out. The enormity of her burden created a formidable mental block. Whatever was troubling her was preventing her to fully articulate her very terrible predicament.

Jake tried to move toward the refrigerator, intending to go get his mom a glass of cold orange juice. But Mary stopped him and motioned him to sit down, alarmed at the sight of the now blood-soaked dressing on her "baby's" left leg.

His mom hurriedly went to the medicine cabinet to get some hydrogen peroxide sterilizing solution, some sterilize gauze, Neosporin, physiological saline, several sticks of cotton swabs, and a pair of scissors. She also got a cup and filled it with semi-hot water from the bathroom faucet. She carefully cut the tape, then delicately took off the dressing and tenderly removed the gauze pads that were atop the still slightly raw wound using a water-moistened cotton swab to loosen the areas where the pads had stuck to the skin. Using a combination of the saline and hydrogen peroxide solutions, along with some sterile pads, she expertly and soothingly cleaned the wound, carefully navigating around the stitches still holding some parts of the raw skin together.

Mary was relieved that no drainage developed around the wound. She applied a moderate amount of the antibiotic, then put moistened pieces of gauze pads over the wound, and, finally, rewrapped the lacerated areas with a new dressing. She gathered up all the old dressing, used pads, used cotton swabs, and the cut tape into a disposable plastic bag, intending to throw them away on her way out of the apartment. But she failed to notice the shiny, metallic sheen of her only son's blood that soaked the used gauze.

Realizing the futility of her awkward attempts in sharing the bad news about her recently-diagnosed medical condition, Mary decided to proceed with plan B. She got a sealed letter that she had laboriously written the night before out of her Gucci bag (one of the few luxuries she indulged in).

The contents of the letter revealed the nature of her diagnosed medical malady, and the fact that it would, in a ninety-nine percent certainty, lead to her demise. Mary hesitantly handed him the unopened note, making her young son promise that he would not read the contents of the letter until exactly three weeks of the coming semestral break had elapsed. She then tightly embraced Jake and planted an affectionate kiss on his forehead. After a while of this, mother and son let go. Mary tried to stifle her sobs, not wanting to roil the boy's mental and emotional state even further. Jake was fighting hard not to let the grimness of the situation affect him.

He surmised that the letter his mother just handed him had bad news written all over it. But his attempt at maintaining a stoic countenance was unsuccessful, as evidenced by the steady stream of tears trickling down his recently-cleaned face. His mom made an abrupt 180-degree turn and walked toward the door. Before leaving the apartment, Mary turned around to blow him three long, affectionate air kisses. In her haste, she forgot to dump the plastic bag containing all those medical wastes into the trash can.

Feeling bone-tired and totally exhausted, JT started to maneuver his growing but skinny five feet and nine point five inches frame into the inviting La-Z Boy leather sofa, but stopped midway. He remembered the letter that his unsettled mom handed him.

In a half-crawling, half-dragging motion, he forced himself to cross the short distance to his backpack and deposited the sealed letter inside, placing the letter so that it was wedged between pages 101 and 102 of his chemistry textbook.

Having safely stored the handwritten note away, he settled snugly into his La-Z Boy sofa. He dozed off almost instantly the moment he laid his head down on the soft, fluffy, monogramed pillow, too exhausted from the all the crazy happenings that went on today.

·········

The last two weeks of the semester came and went without any major surprises. Most of Jake's time was spent at the library, studying and preparing for the final exams. He took his Organic Chemistry 3 and Physics 3 final exams on the last school day of the spring quarter and had turned in his term paper a day before to fulfill the final requirement necessary to pass English 103: composition and critical thinking course.

The only thing holding him back from welcoming the relaxing, carefree summer of 2017 was the thankless chore of packing up his stuff and joining his roommates in cleaning the messy apartment before they could officially vacate.

CHAPTER 14

BFF

One relationship expert opined that a person is extremely lucky if, in that person's lifetime, he or she is able to meet three special friends. These special friends are pretty rare because they have unflinching loyalty; are pillars of strength and power; are beacons of hope; are always looking out for your best interests; are ready to extend a helping hand; are eager listeners and sources of wisdom and guidance; are there to help clean up your mess and by your side as you fight your bloody battles; are ever present to encourage and motivate as you strive to reach the greatness of your God-given talents and potential; are there to serve as a steadying force as you are buffeted by life's ill winds, trials, and tribulations; and are there to help lift you up when you get weighed down by the burdens of daily living.

They cry with you in your moments of grief and pain; suffer with you during your agonizing defeats and abject failures; rejoice with you as you celebrate your successes; and are always willing, able, and committed to see you through the lowest ebbs of life and make sure you emerged from life's crucibles of fire a stronger and a more compassionate being.

....

Jake Timothy was lucky because he found one such friend during his sophomore year at UC San Diego. He met his BFF (best female friend) by accident. Sherry is an indefatigable, enthusiastic, athletic, live wire of a young girl. She is like an Amazon princess, figuratively of course. There was no task, problem, barrier, or challenge that could deter her optimism.

Although she is only one year older than Jake, she is infinitely more mature in her actions and way of thinking. She grew up in the Midwest, living a fun and care-free existence in an idyllic small university town of Ames, Iowa. She is into equestrianism (the Brits have always had the knack of using fancy words)—horseback riding—ever since her Grandpa Bill gifted her with a young colt when she was nine years old. She is quite fond of her magnificent, chestnut-colored horse, whom she affectionately called Prince. She felt exhilaration whenever she prodded Prince into full gallop, both rider and the majestic beast unrestrainedly racing into the wind, going furiously against competitors during an imagined Kentucky Derby run. She occasionally engaged in cosplay, fully geared up and pretending to be one of those highly skilled jockeys competing in the run for the roses.

But it wasn't all fun and games whenever Sherry was at her grandpa's farm. She did a variety of chores, helping in every way she could during the corn-growing and harvesting season. She was such a quick study. She learned to operate both the tractor and the combine harvester by the time she was twelve. She could also fix the small problems periodically besetting those machines. She was quite handy with tools; she patiently and keenly observed Bill while he did the troubleshooting and repair on those monstrous behemoths before trying it on her own.

She attended the nearby Iowa State University, taking up courses that would hopefully earn her a veterinary degree. But she wasn't truly fully committed to that profession yet, since her Grandpa Bill was encouraging her to be an agronomist.

Sherry didn't mind becoming a phytochemist, one who studies the biochemistry of plants, and could envision herself working with her beloved gramps.

But there was one aspect that she intensely disliked about Bill's farming business: the increasing prevalence and abundance of GMO (genetically modified organism) foods. She had read the pros and cons of both sides of the GMO food debate, but as one who had aspirations to be a plant biochemist, she found the fact that profit-oriented megacorporations were manipulating the intent of nature very appalling. Also, it went against the very essence of her being when she heard stories from Bill that mountainous quantities of corn and other crops were periodically burned or destroyed during exceptionally bountiful harvest seasons in order to maintain an economically viable price for those crops. She couldn't understand why those surpluses couldn't be donated to the poor, hungry populace of some Third World countries.

Her dad, David, is a researcher working at a bio-collaborative incubator medical laboratory that was partly supported by the University of California, San Diego. Sherry's parents were divorced, and her dad focused his energies on resveratrol, a naturally occurring compound found in red wine, grapes, raspberries, peanuts, etc.

This polyphenol is known to have antioxidant properties and is being studied for its anticarcinogenic effects. It is reputed to also mitigate the risk of coronary diseases.

But the focus of David's work was resveratrol's potential as an antiaging or cell-rejuvenating miracle drug.

David had called Sherry to invite his free-spirited young daughter to spend the summer of 2016 with him. But since she had already promised to help out her grandpa finish up with the corn-harvesting phase during the summer, she opted to delay her move from Ames to La Jolla until the fall.

She figured she would matriculate at UCSD for the school year 2016-2017. She felt that this would be akin to hitting two birds with one stone: she would get to experience living in a coastal urban university town and get to live and enjoy the company of her tireless dad. By the middle of September 2016, she had completed her migration from the cornfields of Iowa to the bustling harbor town of San Diego. Barely two weeks into the start of the fall quarter, she was already swamped with assignments and weighed down by the specter of looming challenging quizzes and exams.

Sherry had just spent the last six hours studying hard and doing her homework, but the library was closing down in half an hour, so she decided not to wait until the 9:00 p.m. closing time and headed home early. She was about half a block from home and nonchalantly walking along a dimly lighted section of Gilman Drive when she noticed a black Camry seemingly tailing her. She opened the zipper of the front pouch of her dark-blue JanSport backpack and pulled out a handy miniature can of pepper spray. She walked a few more steps in the same southwardly direction, and the car haltingly did the same. She stopped and pulled out her cell phone, pretending to call somebody.

At this point, the driver accelerated and drove past her. Because of the poor lighting in the area, she wasn't able to get a good look at the driver. Sherry felt relieved when the stalker, possibly a drug-crazed rapist, drove away, figuring that she just had narrowly avoided an assault. She was about twenty-three feet from her dad's rented house when the black Camry was back, following her again. With a heightened sense of fear, she felt her heart beating violently, a rush of epinephrine being released by her adrenal glands.

This is a typical reaction by the body in a fight-or-flight situation.

She was quite alarmed at this point, but had the presence of mind to look at both the driver and the vehicle. She had reached the lighted stretch of Gilman Drive and could now clearly see. The driver was a young and handsome teenager, driving a late model black Toyota Camry with a UCSD parking decal. Sherry came to realize that the college student was only trying to find a parking space. So she motioned him to drive his car and follow her as she directed him to her dad's driveway, intending to allow him to park there for a few hours.

Jake expertly glided his car into the driveway, very quickly alighting from the car once he was parked, and profusely thanked the kindhearted lass.

That encounter was instrumental in the beginning of a beautiful friendship.

CHAPTER 15

HELLO AND GOOD-BYE

Ever since that warm, humid, and fateful night in late September, JT and Sher (Sherry's nickname) were inseparable.

Like a true friend that she was, she never bothered to ask what on earth had Jerry been doing driving around looking for a parking spot when, in all probability, he should had an allotted space in the underground parking at the adjacent apartment where he lived. The truth was that he did have his car parked in the slot assigned to him as a resident of the apartment building. But he was feeling the symptoms of the onset of what he suspected to be a viral-caused infection. He was coughing and sneezing, and had sore throat, runny nose, slight headache, and muscle aches. He was thankful that he hadn't develop any fever yet. He was determined to purchase a twenty-count Vicks NyQuil LiquiCaps, hoping to ward off the sickness before it could become something worse. He also needed the sedating effect of the antihistamine doxylamine succinate ingredient present in NyQuil, knowing fully well that he would definitely end up with a sleepless night that was interspersed with bouts of coughing and sneezing unless the sleep-aiding effect of the NyQuil kicked in.

He navigated through the light, leisurely-paced night traffic, reaching the neighborhood Ralphs store in four minutes flat. He grabbed the medicine he needed, making sure that the expiration date was still some months away. He was thrilled to see the self-checkout lines empty. He quickly got the bar code of the NyQuil LiquiCaps scanned and paid with his Chase debit card. He hopped into his newly car-washed black 2015 Toyota Camry and impatiently drove home at about four miles above the speed limit recommended for city driving.

He arrived at this apartment about a half minute faster than the time it took him to get to Ralphs. But once he got to the vicinity of his parking spot, he saw that someone had taken it during the short time he was away, frustrating him. His first instinct was to write the offending driver a note, cursing and berating him or her for callously taking his parking spot. But he decided not to do it and instead opted to park his car on the street. So, the whole episode of driving around in the middle of the night had originated from this irksome situation. But he was thankful for it later on, in that it led to his chance meeting with Sher.

Jake and Sher had spent the last eight months enjoying each other's company. They studied together; they spent a lot of time diligently doing homework and preparing for quizzes and exams. Although they went on occasional trips to McDonald's and Burger King, they did not bother patronizing full-service restaurants like the Outback Steakhouse, TGI Fridays, or Red Lobster. Sherry was a good cook and enjoyed preparing sumptuous meals for an always-hungry Jake.

They watched movies bimonthly, preferring the likes of *Star Wars*, *Mad Max* reboot, the Marvel Super Heroes movies, and *The Fast and the Furious* series. On rare occasions, if Jake found last-minute incredible deals on Stub Hub, they might spend a fun-filled night enjoying a Bruno Mars or a Lady Gaga concert, or a San Diego Padres night game. During the last winter break, they did manage to play a couple of bowling games. Such was the state of their platonic relationship. This charming, adroit girl came into JT's world and made his life a state of limitless and perpetual bliss.

But now, the close friends were feeling depressed. The great times and joyful moments together would soon just be memories forever etched in their hearts and minds. Sher was moving back (for good) to her native

Iowa very soon, while Jake planned to enjoy the lazy days of summer just chilling and hanging out with his Malaysia-born cousin and BMF (best male friend), Matthew.

Jake woke up at 9:00 a.m. the Saturday of the exam week, having just spent the tiresome weekdays taking final exams and submitting a term paper. He was intent on packing all of his stuff and doing his share of cleaning up the apartment before driving to Anaheim to spend a leisurely summer there. He was looking forward to crashing in the bungalow owned by Matthew's mom, and having boisterous fun all summer long with him.

Jake had just started doing the thankless but necessary job when Sher showed up and helped him pack up. The chore was tiresome since Jake had a lot of electronic gadgets, and he wasn't organized in the first place. But due to Sher's superefficient efforts, both the packing and subsequent cleaning of the rented place were done before noon. Jake offered to return the favor but his BFF told him that she was already done collecting and loading her stuff into a rented car.

All good times do come to an end, and the best friends said their long good-byes. They embraced tightly for a seemingly long couple of minutes, kissed each other on the cheeks, tearfully bid one another au revoir, and reluctantly let go. Promises of visiting each other in the future did little to mitigate this highly emotional and painful moment.

CHAPTER 16

VERY UNPALATABLE CHOICES

As Jake was about ready to leave for Anaheim, his cell phone rang. He looked at the screen to identify the caller. It was his dad.

He didn't want to talk to his dad at this particular moment. First, he only had gotten over a hard and trying quarter. Second, he knew that his dad would ask about his grades. He surmised that he would probably end up with a couple of B grades for the core science courses that he took, and his old man would get pissed, since Jerry had high expectations of him. His dad knew Jake had great potential, but that his health wasn't in the best condition.

Some of his symptoms were: being lethargic, always tired, drifting and lacking focus, low immunity (as evidenced by the relative ease with which he had contracted cold and flu viruses), bouts of insomnia, and recurring episodes of IBS (irritable bowel syndrome).

But what drove Jerry batty was his son's tendency to procrastinate, and his terrible habit of cramming for his exams by doing an all-nighter. The combination of all these factors led to his underperforming and, in his old man's words, "Falling way short of your true potential."

JT ignored the call, but Jerry was persistent and he called twice more. JT was hoping that his old man would give up. Instead, he got a text message, saying, *"PICK UP the DARN PHONE!"*

Not wanting to make Jerry any madder, Jake reluctantly answered the fourth call. As expected, after Jerry asked him about the state of his health, he went right to the meat of the matter. His old man asked, "How did you do on your Calculus 3, Physics 3, and Organic Chemistry 3?"

Trying not to rile up his father, deadpan, Jake replied, "The quarter just ended yesterday. My professors haven't had the chance to grade the final exams yet." He felt elated that he was able to parry his dad's question, but was taken aback by what he said next.

"What are your plans for the summer?" Jerry asked.

JT felt his stomach tighten, but still had the good sense to realize that a white lie was the most diplomatic answer to this follow-up question that blindsided him. He knew that the hyper-efficient yet lovable "geezer" would frown on his plans to just chill, enjoy, and hangout with his best buddy Matt. So he blurted out, "I haven't had a chance to think about it."

His answer drove his dad to the wall just the same. Jerry gave him a long spiel about how each grain of sand trickling down the hourglass of time is really a gradual, unstoppable countdown of one's remaining time on this physical world, and about how each of those tiny slivers of irreversible moments is so precious. Ergo, they couldn't just be wasted away needlessly.

JT felt like just hanging up on his old man, because he heard this speech countless of times before. He resisted the impulse, however, not wanting to infuriate Jerry even more. But what came next floored him.

His father gave him three choices to choose from. He could spend the summer doing an eight-week internship working with his dad on his research projects; he could spend his summer learning from his missionary paternal grandparents about religious convictions, about answering God's call, and making the commitment to a lifetime of service; or he could work with Sister Patricia, a Caucasian Catholic nun, to help her manage an orphanage based in the Philippines.

The young, fun-loving underachiever was crestfallen. A mental picture flashed through his mind. He saw himself waving good-bye and blowing air kisses, not to some person but to his plans of enjoying a care-free, boisterous, and pleasure-packed lazy days of summer. Worse, he would need to inform his BMF about this unanticipated and very unpleasant change of plans.

Of course, there was a fourth option that he could exercise, but this would not be a wise move, either. He could say to his dad, "Stop bothering me! Go away! Leave me alone! Let me live my life the way I want to!" But he cared for his dad and didn't want to strain an already distant bond any further. Also, he chose to be extra considerate because Jerry was still recovering from his heart-related episode.

·········

Jerry left his teaching post at the Pasadena City College reluctantly. He relished his role as a compassionate and motivating educator. He felt it an honor and privilege to impart knowledge of chemistry to eager and willing learners. But the most joy he derived in working in this profession was the priceless opportunity to help shape and develop his students' sense of purpose, their societal responsibilities, and the personalities of these future leaders.

He always tried to impart to them the idea of becoming global citizens, that we are all brothers and sisters, all relatives in the literal and figurative sense. To Jerry, we are all descendants of an Omnipotent, Omniscient, and loving Being. In his eyes, the color of one's skin, the country of one's birth, one's economic and social status, and one's religion are artificial distinctions that we had needlessly foisted on all of humanity.

According to the wise old man, if we could collectively gather the willpower and the gumption to destroy these self-defeating demarcations, could learn to coexist peacefully, and would be willing to love each other, then all the hate, the killings, and the unnecessary wars would just disappear.

·········

But after he suffered from a heart condition known as hypertrophic cardiomyopathy, coupled with a chance to do research on life-extending drugs, he decided it was time for a career change.

JT's mom wasn't okay with Jerry's decision. She had been working as a registered nurse at the medical-surgical unit of Kaiser Permanente in Los Angeles. She didn't want herself and the then eleven-year-old Jake to get uprooted and transplanted to a foreign place like Iowa (her grasp of geography was horrible). But Jerry felt that the offer made by an upstart biochemical company affiliated with the Iowa-based Ames Laboratory was just too good to pass up.

So, with both parties unwilling to compromise, Jerry moved to Ames, Iowa, and had been working as a GS-14 level senior researcher for the past six years.

CHAPTER 17

THE MISSIONARY GRANDPARENTS

Answering God's call and committing to a lifetime of becoming His unquestioning and dedicated servant is one of the noblest deeds of all.

To the unbelievers, the supreme act of accepting the call to His service must have occurred under the following scenarios: a) a loaded gun was pointed at the head; b) suffering from a temporary bout of insanity; c) the person was very inebriated; d) the poor, heart-broken person didn't know what else to do; e) a full pardon awaited for previous crimes committed in exchange for this unfathomable action; or f) all of the above.

How else can one explain such an irrational decision? If the question ever gets asked in the *Family Feud*: "What vocation would you want a young kin to be engaged in?" It will be a good bet that "a missionary" is at the bottom of that list.

It takes great courage and deep conviction—no, it takes enlightenment and an inspiration from the Almighty—to make that supreme selfless act. It is not an easy choice to make. An uncommon toughness of character, an unbreakable willpower, an uncompromising stance, and a total obedience to God's call to service are but a few of the requisite qualities necessary to make that ultimate sacrifice.

One of the most famous of this breed of God's servants is Paul the

Apostle. One can study the fifth book of the New Testament, the Acts of the Apostles, for the genesis and purpose of missionary work. But focus on the latter part of the Gospel of Luke (he was an evangelist and companion to Paul) and one can see the beauty and wonder of God's handiwork. It vividly narrates how some of these dedicated proselytizers were chosen and how they were then inspired and moved by an Omniscient Being to do great work.

We are all too familiar with Paul's story. He started as a bad guy. He was on the road to Damascus to apprehend the early disciples/Christians, but was stopped by Jesus (blinded by a great light). Paul was then enlightened about his true calling and became a tireless messenger. He was very instrumental in preaching the Gospel of Christ and the spread of the Christian faith across many diverse regions and far-flung places. Many heathens, unbelievers, and sinners were beneficiaries of his indomitable missionary fervor.

. . . .

The call to spread the Gospel of Jesus about salvation was answered by Jake's paternal grandparents, David and Linda. They had decided, when they were in their mid-twenties, to make that unenviable choice to commit to a lifetime of service. It wasn't an easy choice by any means. They had to uproot themselves from the comforts of home, the warmth and love of family, the luxury of living in a First World country, and willingly moved to the dirt-poor areas of Indonesia. They had to transplant themselves from the vibrant Kansas City to the slum areas of Java, Indonesia. It was a totally different world.

The scoreboard was no longer about how much financial or material wealth a person had accumulated, but rather, how many souls were saved by their dedicated work. Initially, it was a big shock and a rude awakening for Linda. Besides having to make do with less, she was so depressed and helpless at the sight of the plight of these multitudes living in abject poverty. But she learned quickly that in one's life, there is this Omnipotent, All-knowing Being who has a master plan for each and every one of us.

Linda got over any feelings of self-pity swiftly after that realization, graciously accepting the fact that her life was no longer hers and was to be used for the glory of God. She understood why she wanted to become a nurse ever since she was ten years old: her skills and medical knowledge would serve the needy, sick, and impoverished populace of Java, Indonesia.

So it had been this way for JT's grandparents for the past forty-six years. For these two missionaries, their life was consecrated to helping in any way the wretched, destitute people in their daily struggles to survive, and, more importantly, to make them believers in Christ.

For the young Jake Timothy, he knew all too well why his father wanted him to spend his summer in Indonesia. Jerry wanted his teenage son to learn that life should not be centered on material wealth. Jake remembered his old man paraphrasing a verse from the Bible: "For what good is it, if you gain all the riches in this world but you lost your soul in the process?"

Jerry's whole objective was for JT to build on his moral fiber, and to acquire—hopefully by observing and through osmosis—a compassionate, caring, and loving heart.

CHAPTER 18

THE ORPHANAGE

O ften times, things get tarried and a person becomes impatient. But in the fullness of time, if it is in accordance with the Almighty's plan, then all these will come to pass and come into being.

. . . .

Such was the case with the spacious, nipa-thatched shelter located behind a fish pond that functions so perfectly as an orphanage. There was never an intended plan to build this Heaven-sent gift.

Sister Patricia is a Catholic nun, identified with the religious Sisters of the Sacred Heart. She had been rounding up the strays, the abandoned kids and the homeless, who were loitering and whiling away in the neighborhood. She did her charity work and compassionate deeds in the agricultural part of Dela Paz, Laguna.

. . . .

Dela Paz is a sub-urban annex of Biñan. The City of Biñan itself is located about twenty-one miles south of Manila (the capital city) and has a population approaching 400,000. There are still farms dotting the outskirts of the city, although evidence of industrialization is sprouting everywhere. It is not uncommon to see among the frontage of endless rows of agricultural land, suddenly appearing in plain sight is the ubiquitous McDonald's, situated right alongside a newly built mini-mall.

It is an unfortunate conversion of much-needed farmland into commercial strip centers, restaurants, and fast-food joints. But it is not only this type of transformation that has been ongoing.

A recent transaction that had members of the farmers' cooperative up in arms involved a plot of agricultural land sold by the owner who migrated to Canada.

He had liquidated most of his assets at cheap prices due to his haste to move abroad. The real estate agent found a ready and able buyer for a plot of farmland, a rich businessman who offered a mutually agreeable price. Manny, a Manila-based Chinese Filipino astute in the *art of the deal*, facilitated the closing of the deal, agreeing to an all-cash mode of payment. What riled up the local farmers was the new landlord's plan for the piece of land. Manny had purchased the property not for the planting of an important staple food source, rice, but for the construction of a tilapia farm. Due to an ever-increasing Filipino population, coupled with these greed-motivated, mind-boggling, and wanton conversions of agricultural land, the Philippines has seen a role reversal. Three decades ago, the country had a huge surplus of rice, making it a top rice-exporting nation. Nowadays, this Asian country needs huge shipments of the this staple food sourced from Vietnam and Thailand.

Locals were quite upset at this unmitigated, irreversible, and increasing pace of agri-land conversion. Sadly, the Filipino government took no actions, preferring a policy of laissez-faire. Initially, the actions were peaceful protests and picketing. When these methods didn't work, stone-throwing incidents directed at the construction site, harassments of workers (at the site), coupled with threats of bodily harm were tried next. But what brought things to a boil was the attempted abduction of the construction foreman. Although it was unsuccessful, it did temporary brought the construction of the fish pond to a halt. But both sides knew this was just a brief respite from the nasty stuff going on.

Entrepreneurs get rich because of their tenacity and business acumen. But this mixed-breed magnate is much more than that. He is both compassionate and an outside-the-box thinker. He didn't go with the fight-fire-with-fire route. Instead of hiring the meanest goons he could find to fight the protesters, vandals, and would-be kidnappers, he chose to take the high road. He prayed hard for guidance and wisdom. After many days of contemplation and deliberation, he decided on a course of action. He would build a peace offering. The unused part of the fish farm, located at the back of the lot, would become the site of an *orphanage*.

. . . .

Imagine the mixed emotions that ran through Sister Pat's (her nickname) head. When Manny asked his trusted aide to fetch the nun, she couldn't help but speculate why. Did one or two boys under her ward do some mischiefs again? When Manny told her about his plan to put up a large, spacious orphanage at the back lot of the fish farm, she was dumbfounded. She burst into tears of joy, tightly shaking the benefactor's hand first, followed by an awkward hug, all the while, thanking this generous soul over and over again.

This is better than manna from Heaven. While the free food from above fed the Israelites during their wanderings in the desert, this gift-wrapped, Heaven-sent shelter would prevent the orphans and the homeless from meandering aimlessly, for these poor abandoned kids would now have a place to call their own. Sister Pat was still in a state of shock one hour after receiving the good news.

Why?

She had been supplicating in her twice-a-day prayers for just such a permanent place for a growing number of disadvantaged and needy kids, whom she was caring for in the past several years.

CHAPTER 19

A CRUEL MISTRESS

There was an uneasy peace that descended among the tilapia aquaculture group and the neighboring farmers. Even with the announced intent of constructing an orphanage, both sides only interacted when necessary, treating each other with a healthy dose of suspicion and disdain. The good thing was that no further untoward incident occurred after the attempted abduction. Each day that passed unfolded the steady progress in the construction of the much-needed shelter for the orphaned kids.

Simultaneously developing was the aqua farm project. The fish pond was slowly but surely taking shape. In light of these developments, relations between both groups became less frosty and were showing signs of guarded optimism. After four months, the culmination of the twin projects was a sight to behold: a fully functional fish pen, ready for the rearing of tilapia fingerlings, coexisting with a very spacious utilitarian shelter.

The constructed orphanage might be inelegant and spartan, but in conjunction with the fish farm, the two created a symphony even the New York or Vienna Philharmonic couldn't rival. The aqua farm provided the fish for the hungry kids' daily nourishment, while the orphanage provided these young, impoverished souls educational and spiritual sustenance. There was this masterful orchestral performance unfolding. The fish farm provided the "feed them for a day" part, but equally important, the orphanage did the nurturing and teaching of these helpless kids, contributing the "teach them how to fish, then you feed them for a lifetime" component.

London Symphony Orchestra, join us in saluting a newly arrived, highly capable competitor!

After a well-attended and much-publicized benediction by Father Art Rosales, a priest from the local parish, both the fish pond and the orphanage buckled down for business. The fish-rearing cycle could typically take between four to five months, but the hungry kids got their allocation of tasty fillets from undersized or sickly fish, the trimming of the population of these fresh water creatures due to exceedingly high stocking density, disposal of wounded or picked-upon tilapias, etc.

The aqua farm avoided the hatchery part of the business, preferring to focus its energy on the growing out of the young fingerlings into full-sized, commercially-desirable tilapias.

The younger kids residing in the back-lot shelter derived much pleasure and thrills in watching these "mini-boogers with tails" swimming and racing each other furiously.

The ultimate goal of the business side of this aquaculture was to bring the fingerlings to marketable size (typically around 0.75 to 0.95 pounds) in an economically viable and most profitable way. Sister Pat had, by then an odd mix of some thirty-plus young children and teens. Roughly half of these were orphans, while the rest were the abandoned, the runaways, ex-rugby sniffers, or ex-street beggars.

. . . .

Rugby is a brand name for a contact cement, the chemical fumes of which are reputed to cause the persons who sniff them a temporary high. Interviews with the "rugby boys" revealed a disturbing reason behind their inclination to do such an idiotic thing. They claimed that being in this fleeting, solvent-manufactured, reality-suspending state allows to escape from the hunger pangs that they oftentimes couldn't satisfy. The sad reality is that this pathetically unwise move leave these poor souls addicted, and more prone to commit crimes.

This sad plight, coupled with their need for money to finance their debasing addiction, leads them stuck deep in an odious pile of dog excrement. Such is only an example of situations afflicting the needy and downtrodden in many Third World countries, where there are no safety nets and almost nonexistent assistance from the government. The term "starved to death" is a literal possibility for multitudes of poverty-stricken masses.

....

Blissful and harmonious situations don't last forever, but the twin disasters that struck literally one after the other exemplified the fact that fate can be such a cruel mistress.

Barely two months after both projects came to fruition, a weird weather phenomenon, centered primarily around a two-mile radius, occurred with such devastating force (inexplicable violent torrents of water rained down mercilessly, coupled with ninety-five miles per hour winds), lasting twelve long minutes. Much of the nipa material used for the roofing was blown away, many areas of the orphanage were flooded, and some wood panels were destroyed.

But the most damaging aspect was reserved for the fish pond. A mysterious, oxygen-depleting event asphyxiated many of the 12,000 tilapias being raised in the pond.

CHAPTER 20

THE DEDICATED STAFF

A lesser man not blessed with an iron will, dogged determination, and a stubborn refusal to admit defeat would graciously and humbly accepted the unavoidable conclusion that the twin projects were both abject failures. But Manny isn't. He is built on steely inner strength and oozing self-confidence; he regards setbacks like these to be merely equivalent to working on complex crossword puzzles, solvable with the application of requisite brainpower. In much simpler terms, the wealthy magnate relishes the opportunity to meet the challenges presented by these types of difficult situations.

This temporary setback, according to this wise and experienced tycoon, is the easiest to solve. Any problem that required monetary solution could be taken care of in a jiffy. In this Chinese Filipino's mind, the amount of material wealth is nothing but a scorecard, a rough indicator of the successful implementations of interrelated sequential business decisions. Once a person earned enough to pay for the necessities of daily living and occasional indulgences of luxury, in Manny's opinion, these excess amounts owned are just differentiated by the number of zeros trailing after a nonzero digit, sitting in a dusty vault somewhere or in some pitifully low-interest-paying bank accounts. The pious and devoted Christian sincerely believed that he is but an appointed steward of this material wealth. That was the reason why he had no qualms about donating huge sums to charities, NGOs (nongovernmental organizations), and causes he supported. Money could be earned, could be spent, and could be lost, so it didn't bother him one bit if the numbers on the scoreboard moved upward or downward. He had such supreme confidence in his business acumen, so much so that according to an oft-told tale of his famous boast: "Put me in an isolated island, equipped with nothing but my razor-sharp mind, and I will not only survive but will thrive in that desolate, trying environment."

The repair of the damaged orphanage and restocking of the fish farm occurred in military-styled efficiency, needing only the passage of eight Earth days. It is in these very type of categorically disastrous situations that the innate goodness of humanity shows up. The well-known and almost uniquely Filipino term *Bayanihan* (loosely translated as spirit of community and cooperation) moved hundreds of people, volunteering to help clean up, fix, and rebuild. The unity of purpose and the magnificence of the power of volunteerism were in full display.

The end result of this community spirit was quite evident and stunning. One only needed to look at the spruced-up shelter. It was an improved and more aesthetically pleasing version of the original!

....

Choosing the right personnel who were inspired by Sister Pat's vision and passion resulted in the formation of a highly organized structure that operated in such admirable and superb efficiency. The successful managing of the shelter required the creativeness, boundless energy, and total dedication of all the leaders and staff, so it was both divine-assisted and fortuitous that the right personnel were committed to this noble work.

Listed below are the names of inspired and dedicated leaders and teachers, alongside the names of the capable and efficient employees and young helpers: Sister Pat, the tireless and very adept administrator, who also taught religion and faith. Bong Ramirez, the husband of Delia, a

University of the Philippines (UP) biology graduate who set the curriculum and taught science and math subjects. Delia Ramirez, also a UP graduate, who handled the other topics not taught by her husband. Julie, Sister Pat's dependable and capable assistant. Rey, the young, skinny, and tall orphan who served as the liaison to the fish farm personnel. Jon-Jon, the very friendly young boy who went to the market three blocks away every morning to solicit vegetable and the occasional meat donations from vendors and butchers. Mark, the jovial abandoned teen who were friends with many of the workers at a nearby chicken farm. And Juanito, aka (also known as) Jani, the assigned leader of the group of orphans and misfits, tasked to clean up and to do other custodian responsibilities.

CHAPTER 21

THE CHICKEN FARM

Situated not even a block west of the orphanage is a stinky chicken farm. On thick humid days, when the gentle wind blew the air eastward, the kids inside the orphanage complained of the tear-jerking, foul-smelling, ammonia-laced odor of chicken manure. But it wasn't only the nitrogenous amines that were totally responsible for the fetid stench. The decaying residue of digested food left in the chicken feces mixed with some volatile organic compounds produced by the bacterial colonies in the poop also contributed to the terribly suffocating odor.

Unlike the strong opposition demonstrated against the conversion of the agri-land to the fish farm, this poultry farm, while not warmly welcomed by any means, was allowed to be built (reluctantly). The owners of the chicken farm were more sophisticated and unquestionably public relations (PR) savvy. Even before construction of the farm commenced, its personnel went around the neighboring rice farms, promising availability of dirt-cheap, dried pelletized chicken manure once the farm was up and running.

. . . .

The dried fowl poop is reputed to be a much superior source (vis-a-vis that of horse, cow, or deer dung) of nitrogen, phosphorus, and potassium. It is also a good soil supplement since it adds the necessary organic compounds-originated nutrients and beneficial biota, and increases the water-holding capacity of the soil. For those not in the planting and harvesting business, biyearly community gatherings and fun parties are promised. These will feature exciting contests like juggling of eggs, eating the most eggs (come join the fun: Joey Chestnut, Takeru Kobayashi, and Miki Sudo) in a ten-minute span, carrying eggs with a spoon held by the mouth while racing to a finish line, and so on.

The pledge of free food, free booze, fun parties, entertaining contests, and supply of rock-bottom-priced chicken excrement as fertilizers for their farms guaranteed the quiet, unenthusiastic acquiescence to the unappealing project.

It was how the egg farm was reluctantly allowed to come to existence.

The official term for the business is layer poultry farming. It is an enterprising business of raising egg-laying fowls for the purpose of collecting and selling the eggs commercially. This business runs on roughly seventy-five-week cycle: raising day-old chicks into seventeen-week-old pullets into egg-laying (from week eighteen or nineteen to week seventy-five) hens, and then selling the unproductive old hens (at the end of the seventy-five-week cycle) as ready source of the tasty chicken satay, etc. After a brief period of decontamination and rigorous cleaning of the farm, the whole cycle can be repeated over again.

The possible differences in the myriad of enterprises engaged in this egg-producing business has to do with the color of eggs produced and the scale/scope of the venture. While in this country, white eggs are preferred by a wide margin compared to brown eggs, it is the total opposite in most Southeast Asian countries. There, white eggs are not as commercially desired as the brown eggs. Somehow, it is etched in the minds of the people in these regions that the brown-shell-encased embryos are more nutritious.

But numerous studies came out with similar myth-busting facts:

exactly same servings of calories, identical amount of proteins, vitamin B, and cholesterol are found in both varieties.

Maybe the incorrect assumption came about due to the more expensive price (relative to white eggs) of brown eggs, and the fallacy of the logic: more expensive, ergo, more nutritious. But the fact of the matter is that brown eggs are more expensive only because the cost of producing them is higher. Why? Hens that lay brown eggs are bigger and consume more food, driving up the cost per brown egg, which then gets reflected in the higher price.

Another notable difference would be how the seventy-five-week cycle is conducted. Smaller, less capitalized businesses will run the cycle about once every eighteen months, while megacorporations might acquire a much bigger place and divide it into four quadrants, and then run four cycles concurrently but at a staggered start. That way, there is always a continuous, uninterrupted fresh-egg production.

....

For this particular layer farm, the owner decided to do a more expensive but shorter variation of the cycle. Instead of starting with one-day-old chicks, he purchased 70,000 fourteen-week-old pullets from a reputable and established company. He allowed the pullets to mature into eighteen-week-old egg-laying hens in his chicken farm, enabling these fowls to adjust and acclimatize to their new environment. These rapidly maturing pullets were placed on a rapid, growth-inducing concoction of starter feed, feed supplements, proteins, mineral, and vitamins. When these reach the eighteen-week egg-laying stage, layer poultry feed supplant the starter feed as one of their important source of nourishment. The egg-laying stage start at week eighteen and end around week seventy-five (although some might still lay eggs until week seventy-eight). The maximum egg-laying capability peak at week twenty-six and start tapering off gradually. Daily production of 50,000 brown eggs commencing at week twenty-six wasn't too uncommon. Some key personnel of the layer poultry farm:

- Patrick aka "the chief," supervised his crew of fourteen, ensuring smooth running of the farm
- Jessie, Patrick's dependable assistant
- Ricarte aka Karte, the security guard
- Roberto aka Berto, the best friend of Mark (the jovial kid from the orphanage)
- Dominic, the lazy and ill-tempered worker responsible for gathering up the chicken manure and processing them; also an incorrigible bully
- Anita, the gentle lady who managed the cafeteria
- Melchior aka Mel, the veterinary student responsible for the health of the 70,000 egg-laying hens

CHAPTER 22

THE DECISION

This chapter is the continuation of the events in Chapter 16.

In JT's opinion, all three choices offered to him weren't really any good. He loved his paternal grandparents, David and Linda, having met them two or three times while they were on their respite back in the States. Both loving grandparents made it a point to try to drop by and visit the growing JT no matter how hectic or how short their biennial break from missionary work was. They fascinated him with stories about the joys and perils of spreading the Gospel of Christ to the poor people of Java, Indonesia. It was an especially hard task to preach and try to bring these poor people into the fold of Christianity.

....

Islam is the major religion in Indonesia, with approaching ninety percent of the population being its adherents. That means there are about 225 million Muslims (also spelled as Moslems) in that country. But at least present-day missionaries no longer face the life-extinguishing predicaments that early missionaries suffered.

Paul was martyred via decapitation for his unwavering faith even in the face of death, and the stories of persecutions and executions of missionaries along with their Christian converts in sixteenth-century Japan are all too familiar. But it is a major challenge nonetheless, a very difficult test of one's mettle and deep religious conviction to proselytize in a place steeped in Islamic culture and beliefs. It is made exceedingly more difficult by the uncompromising message of Christianity: that *Jesus is the only way to salvation.*

While this Gospel truth is deeply rooted and backed by Jesus' own words in John 14:6 (NKJV): "I am the way, the truth and the life. No one comes to the Father except through me," it makes it a difficult proposition. For how can a person, indoctrinated and immersed in zealous Islamic teachings, suddenly just do a 180-degree turn and blindly accept the fact that salvation is only accorded to Christian believers? But the Lord works in mysterious ways.

. . . .

Through David and Linda's compassionate nature, their dedication, through "action, not words," through their tender care of the needy, through their overflowing love for the downtrodden and poverty-stricken populace, these missionaries became very capable "fishers of men (and women)."

Jake, however, quickly struck this option off his list. He knew that he had neither the religious convictions nor the talent necessary to do this spreading of the good news about salvation, which left him with two equally unappealing choices: Either he spend the next six weeks helping the tireless nun run the Philippine-based orphanage or a summer internship working with his old man in researching life-extending drugs.

He spent the next several days contemplating and weighing both options. After utilizing many long and hard hours of exhaustive and careful deliberation, he finally arrived at a decision. But unlike that famous, multitalented basketball superstar who had the capability to announce his intentions in front of a nationwide audience, JT could only relay his decision, rather meekly, via a text message to his dad.

The dejected teenager was taking his meager talents and sorry behind not to the exciting coastal SoBe (nickname for South Beach), but to the boring, suburban Dela Paz.

His text to his dad Jerry read: *"Please let Sister Pat know I will be helping out at the orphanage."*

The motivating factor that made him choose this option was his health. He didn't think he could stand the rigors and demands of working under a slave-driver father. Not only was Jerry very meticulous and exacting, he demanded the absolutely right thought processes or justifications for any course of action. It was always an intense atmosphere, which could be likened to defending a doctoral thesis.

On the other hand, he could mix fun, play, chilling out, and work while babysitting the young ones at the orphanage.

CHAPTER 23

DEAR UNCLE REGGIE

JT was quite happy when he was met by his Uncle Reginald at the Cebu International Airport. He was very shocked to see how his mom's brother had aged so fast, wildly speculating that the intense, competitive pressure of being in the copra business must be having this life-shortening effects on him.

Reggie is an astute businessman. He also owns several mini-marts and is a franchisee of a popular Filipino pharmacy giant. But he lets his Filipina wife May manage the twelve mini-marts and seven pharmacy stores. Reggie is content to focus on his extensive copra trading business and his growing real estate portfolio. Yet the intricacies and vagaries of this ultracompetitive business could be more than enough to drive even seasoned traders batty.

. . . .

In agricultural commodities trading, there are so many variables and unexpected occurrences that can greatly affect profits and losses. Some of the following factors can make the price of copra fluctuate wildly: weather conditions, supply coming from foreign sources, bountiful or poor harvest, prices of this commodity in neighboring countries, number of typhoons or hurricanes hitting the coconut plantations, frequency and scope of coconut tree infestations, worldwide spot price of pure coconut oil (extracted from copra using expeller or cold-press technique), possible aflatoxins contamination in improperly dried copra, and many more.

Essentially, any of these factors affects the supply-and-demand economics of copra. But there are also some other situations that can potentially bankrupt even an experienced trader. An example of which is narrated below.

At the start of the season, a trader needs to advance substantial amounts of money to many small, undercapitalized coconut farmers, as necessary funds for nurturing, irrigating, fertilizing, and de-infesting of coconut-yielding trees, as well as for planting of young trees, etc. Basically, the trader underwrites the expenses associated with inducing the trees to yield a substantial number of coconuts, which then gets turned into copra. The only way for the trader to recoup the money advanced, plus some expected profits, is for the coco farmer to turn around and sell the copra to the same trader at an agreed-upon price at the end of the harvest (allowing for subsequent processing of coconuts to copra) season. These types of transactions rely heavily on an element of trust. Sadly, not a few of these farmers can be dishonest and untrustworthy. You can just think of various permutations of misplaced trust. Taken together or in some combinations of these can lead to utter ruin. In short, one has to make this type of risky business decision every coco season. One can just imagine the ulcer-causing moments experienced by helpless traders, all the while trying to convince themselves into believing that they entrusted those substantial amounts of money to the right group of coco farmers. But things don't always turn out as expected.

. . . .

There were years when Reggie's gut instincts failed him and he suffered considerable losses. But the extremely profitable years more than offset the bad years, and as a whole, this dread-filled business made him a wealthy man. The only bad collateral damage was that, by engaging in this anxiety-filled trading, Reggie aged prematurely.

In his excitement in meeting his uncle, JT initially failed to notice the two large, muscular men standing some five feet away, squarely behind his uncle. After finally becoming aware of these two men, JT took a good look at them and could vividly see the contour of some segment of a handle (definitely indicative of concealed firearm) on the lower right portion of the shirt of each men. His uncle read the puzzled look on his nephew's face, so he explained the need for the services of two armed bodyguards. Reggie was a trusting person before the incident that he was about to narrate to his young nephew.

A rival copra trader had informed Reggie of an incredible deal being offered by a group of coco farmers who needed to raise funds pronto due to unpaid loans from the local bank. These farmers were willing to liquidate 65,000 kilos of copra at fifteen percent below the prevailing market price; the stipulations were that the sale had to be consummated that same day and in an all-cash transaction. Reggie's rival mentioned that he wasn't able to raise the necessary cash to take advantage of this great deal, but that he was willing to pass this along contingent on a zero point five percent finder's fee.

Reginald graciously thanked the other trader for this opportunity and promised to reward him with the fee once the transaction was finished. He quickly went to a local bank to withdraw the cash needed. He was halfway to the town where the coco farmers were supposed to be waiting when he encountered a roadblock put up by several men toting automatic weapons. They forced him off his vehicle and started beating him up. One of the goons scampered up his late-model Toyota Land Cruiser and looked for something. He found Reggie's blue duffel bag and alighted from the Japanese-made car. This bad dude then opened up the bag and expressed feigned surprise at the sight of thirty bundles of 1,000-peso bills. The bad guys then huddled together, in all probability discussing the copra trader's fate.

Before the evil men had a chance to carry out Reggie's execution, a big Isuzu heavy-duty truck approached, the passengers shouting and cursing and making all sorts of noises. This commotion scared off the villains and they scattered in different directions. The perfectly timed arrival of Reggie's workers, whom he had previously instructed to ferry the sixty-five tons of copra, saved his life. Yes, he lost 3,000,000 pesos that horrible day, but the trader was feeling fortunate that he got to live another day. Fearing a repeat of this ugly and scary incident, his friend the mayor sent two ex-soldiers to serve as Reggie's personal bodyguards.

His rich uncle booked JT for a week's stay at Shangri-La hotel. After letting the eager teen rest a day from the effects of jet lag, Reggie delivered on his promise to be a gracious host. Tourists spots like the Taoist Temple, Magellan's Cross, Mactan Channel, Basilica del Santo Niño, Fort San Pedro, and Cathedral Museum were some of the places they visited. To satisfy JT's fine gastronomical cravings, eateries like Anzani, Circa 1900, Kanyeon Yakiniku, Zubuchon, Garden Cafe were patronized.

On the eve of his departure for the orphanage, Jake's Uncle Reggie took him to a popular karaoke bar, and the two now fully bonded amigos really had a heck of time.

This Cebu-based relative of his sure knew how to give this maturing teenager an unforgettable time of his young life.

CHAPTER 24

FOUNDLINGS, ORPHANS, RUNAWAYS, STRAYS, AND THE "RUGBY" BOYS

When Sister Pat chose to commit to a lifetime of service, she decided to focus her energy on the most vulnerable segment of society: the innocents. These were the young, who, through no fault of their own, or in their desire to escape from untenable domestic situations, and at the worst possible moment of their lives, were left alone in this physical world.

They were devoid of parental guidance; lacking in familial warmth and care; helpless and unable to fend for themselves; untrained in skills necessary to eke out daily living; negligible spiritual growth; low self-confidence, low self-esteem, and low sense of dignity; and the worst thing, rejected and unloved. This miserable group included the orphaned, the misfits, the strays, the runaways, the rejects, the abandoned, the street urchins, the "rugby boys," and the outcasts. Although these innocents hadn't suffered the same heart-rending fate as those felled by the murderous Herod's edict (Matthew 2:16), in Sister Pat's eyes, doing nothing for them was tantamount to dooming them to the same unfortunate fate.

She consecrated her life to serve the helpless and vulnerable innocents by feeding and nurturing them, educating them, building their confidence and self-esteem, encouraging their spiritual growth, creating for them an atmosphere of care and love to help them develop a compassionate heart, making them learn about their societal and social responsibilities, and helping them realize the true purpose of their existence.

It was this lifelong mission that she had been diligently and steadfastly trying to accomplish for the last twenty-five years. She still couldn't believe the two miracles that just recently transpired: the unexpected arrival of Bong and Delia, especially when both committed to teach the children those subjects in general education, and the heaven-sent multipurpose and homey orphanage.

Sister Pat now had a very efficient and dependable staff in place, supporting her in running this nurturing, love-filled shelter. She considered herself very fortunate to have someone to delegate certain chores.

Julie is such a person, an indispensable and responsible assistant. She is the accidental result of a supposedly strictly business transaction between a young, lustful American serviceman and a local Filipina who was engaged in the most ancient profession in the world. It wasn't even clear whether the young soldier was part of a contingent that was stationed in the now-shuttered US Naval Base Subic Bay in Olongapo City or part of a covert group that might had stayed after the base was closed down. Since her mom was always busy practicing her craft, Julie was placed under the care of her maternal grandmother living in Dela Paz, which was a good thing because her grandma was a very kind, loving, and a pious woman. This was the reason why Julie turned out to be an upright, conservative, caring, and dependable lass despite the circumstances. Everything was going so well until her grandma passed away unexpectedly when she was eighteen, and with nobody to turn to, she ended up having to wake up early each day to sell *sampaguita* (the national flower of the Philippines) garlands near the entrance of the nearby church. Taking pity on her, Sister Pat invited Julie to join her at the orphanage.

Julie is blessed in a lot of ways despite how she came into being.

Although she never got to know her American father, she continued to dream that one day, somehow, somewhere, she would get the chance to meet him. One would think that she might end up working the same profession as her mom or that she would definitely end up with morally decadent values, but fate intervened. Her grandma brought her up to become a virtuous, morally upright, dependable, religious, and loving person.

Her features are a prime example of that wonderful fusion between the best qualities of Caucasian and Asian genes.

In short, she is quite the stunner.

CHAPTER 25

My Boot Camp

Jake's Uncle Reggie was nice enough to travel with him up north and dropped him off at the orphanage. They were met by Sister Pat and her very capable assistant, Julie. The usual handshakes, greetings, and pleasantries were exchanged. But the young JT couldn't help but be mesmerized by the exquisite beauty in front of him. In fact, if his uncle didn't gently nudge him, he might not have let go of the young woman's delicate hands when they were shaking hands. That would have been a very embarrassing moment, for the both of them.

Strangers in the night... the musical thought running through Jake's head.

The nun instructed Julie to familiarize JT with the structural and operational details of the orphanage, as well as to provide him with a daily list of chores and responsibilities to do for the next six weeks. Before the nun moved on to attend to other matters, she asked the guests if they had any questions.

Jake had been curious about how his dad got to know the Catholic nun, so he timidly asked, "How did you and my dad get to know each other?"

The kind nun recalled a rainy day in July of last year, when a very soaked mid-fifties man walked into the reception area. Jani (the teen responsible for cleaning and other custodian responsibilities) was trailing the man, imploring him to dry himself up with a towel, which was held patiently by Jon-Jon, another ward, before going inside the orphanage. But the impatient ex-professor ignored his plea and kept walking toward the reception area. Jani was pissed at the sight of the little puddles of water left all over the floor, essentially marking the path where the middle-aged man had traversed as he moved from the entrance to the insides of the orphanage. With a resigned sigh, Jani grabbed the mop and the presser to clean up the watery mess. Alerted by Jani's loud pleadings, Sister Pat came out. She saw the dripping-wet gent, grabbed the towel from Jon-Jon's hands, and helped dry the still-wet guest.

After thanking the kindly vestal, he introduced himself as Jerry and explained the purpose of his visit. It turned out that the ex-professor heard about the existence of this orphanage, learned also about the nice and commendable ministry that it did with its young wards. He was visiting since he wanted to know what kinds of books this center of learning needed. Jerry had good working relationship with book reps and could get older-edition books at minimal cost. The nun thanked him; they exchanged business cards and Jerry was then introduced to Bong and Delia, to work out the details of the planned books transaction. A little over a year later, the bookshelves of the library of the orphanage were overflowing, crammed with gazillions of books on many diverse topics and genres.

Reggie left JT in the care of the indefatigable nun, and the maturing young man was instructed to follow the stunning Julie to her cubicle.

While there, the two discussed his chores and responsibilities, going over a to-do checklists, broken down into daily, weekly, and monthly lists. The efficient assistant also gave him a schedule listing the times and type of activities that the young juveniles of the orphanage engaged in on a Monday to Friday timeframe.

JT thought, *Oh, no! I just signed up to help run a boot camp for retards and rejects!* Fearing that the American Asian beauty might somehow read his mind, he tried to quickly banish the rude thought.

ELIXIR

After Jake was given a detailed picture of the chores and scope of his responsibilities, he was led to his sleeping quarters. He was to bunk with Mark, a jovial abandoned teen. After Julie left, Jake felt tired and decided to just lie down on his small bed (well, the bed wasn't long enough to accommodate his 5'9.5" frame).

Julie was mortified when she dropped by an hour later and found Jake still lying on his bed, drifting to sleep. Jake jumped out of the bed quickly when he saw the shocked expression that registered on that elegant face. Julie had expected the handsome teen to have unpacked, showered (or at least washed to refresh himself), and ready to get started with his assigned chores. It was quite a letdown to her when she saw JT just lazing about.

JT blushed, and some areas of his cheeks turned dark pink. He sheepishly remarked, "Oh, I thought I can have the afternoon off."

Julie tried to tell him about the place needing to be ran efficiently, and that no lazy bums were allowed, but was interrupted by an accusing question him.

"You don't like me, do you?" JT looked hard into her eyes and tried to get a "tell" from her body language.

Two less lonely people... once more, a musical thought came unbidden in Jake's mind.

When two equally beautiful beings meet, the animal magnetism and strong attraction for each other become overwhelming.

....

An analogy in sports is: When Rafa Nadal was contending against a worthy opponent in Roger Federer (this was especially true some years back, when both were in their primes); when the smallish but gutsy Filipino pugilist Pacquiao was battling Mexican warriors Morales and Marquez; or when Magic was competing for the championships against Larry.

In all three instances, these hard-core competitors, all alpha males, relished the chance of competing against the best of the best. After engaging in hard-fought battles, each opponent has nothing but respect and admiration for their equally gifted, worthy adversary.

....

So it was with these two wonders of creation. God must had been in one of His very inspired moods when he created magnificent earthen vessels for these modern-day versions of the irresistible Adonis and the enchanting Venus. Two equally alluring specimens of beauty, magically drawn to each other and instantly becoming honorary members of each other's mutual-admiration society.

Not wanting to lie, Julie confided to him, "Your dad requested that we give you a rigid, activities-filled, and responsibilities-laden workload while you are here. He doesn't want you goofing around or just whiling your time away."

At this point, Jake was floored and didn't know whether to laugh or cry. He now realized the irony of ironies.

First, he tried to literally run away from his old man by choosing not to work in his lab. But the 8,000-mile-distance failed to stop the ex-professor from extending his influence. Second, it now dawned on him that he wasn't here to help run a boot camp. Rather, his daddy dearest had just enrolled him in a six-week Philippine-based *boot camp*!

CHAPTER 26

FUN AT THE CHICKEN FARM

JT decided to work his butt off doing the chores assigned to him, and to fulfill his responsibilities diligently for two main reasons: One, he didn't want the orphanage kids to say that this *Amboy* (the name they teasingly called him, shortened from American Boy) was a lazy, no-good bum; two, he wanted to impress Julie.

So he was always toiling away, inspired and looking forward to lunchtimes and siesta breaks. It was at those times when this youthful Adonis and the effervescent Venus huddled together and enjoyed every moment in each other's company. He couldn't even remember the details of the anecdotes, jokes, or stories that they shared, since everything was so hazy and blurred when he tried to recall. All he could remember, feel, and hear were the sounds of laughter, the happiness, and the immense euphoric state he felt whenever they were together.

The *Amboy* was on cloud nine, and more than ready to fall in love.

One could just imagine that pesky and mischievous little tyke with the cherubic face and miniature wings getting ready to shoot those tiny love-tipped arrows at these two mutually-infatuated youngsters.

When I need you...

All work and no play was no fun, either. Sundays were when everything work-related ground to a halt. Attending Sunday-morning worship was highly encouraged. But the most fun happened in the afternoon: trips to the newly constructed mall, going to the movies, playing sports like basketball or racing or singing contests between preformed groups of youngsters of the orphanage.

But for this Sunday afternoon, JT, Mark and a few more of the kids had plans for a different kind of fun: a friendly competition.

Jake found a new buddy in Mark, an abandoned teen who was quite jovial and had a happy-go-lucky personality. Mark had a lot of friends, especially those workers at the neighboring chicken farm. For this particular afternoon, some of the teenagers from the orphanage would engage in a series of friendly contests against the workers of the chicken farm.

There would definitely be some unannounced side bets, but for the most part, this organized event was done in the spirit of fun and camaraderie. The categories include synchronized racing to a finish line with an uncooked egg held between the foreheads of a duo of teammates, racing to a finish line with raw egg placed on a spoon that was held in place by biting the utensil with the teeth, nudging an egg toward a predetermined line using only one's nose (no hands please!), throwing raw eggs for the farthest distance without breaking them, and eating the most number of boiled eggs.

...Run...for...the...roses...

All the contestants from both groups had been looking forward to this competition; everyone was EGG-cited!

Anita, the cafeteria lady, was gracious in offering to prepare and get those eggs ready. Say what you want about Jake Timothy: lazy kid, time-waster, loafer, procrastinator, underachiever. These might be apt descriptions of him, but one trait you couldn't imagine he possessed was his super-competitive nature; he hated to lose.

Sensing that the contest might boil (figuratively, no pun intended) down to the egg-eating part as being the tie-breaker event, Jake prepared and wanted to put himself in a position to win the joust (just in case, but his sixth sense was presciently urging him to get ready for just such a possibility). What he did next was akin to what the fictional legendary

Captain James T. Kirk (any relations to JT?) did when he was subjected to a simulated testing under stressful conditions. But whereas the resourceful captain reprogrammed the simulation so he couldn't fail, this ultracompetitive youngster, to help him get a big leg up against the competition, skipped his dinner the night before so that he would be famished by the time the contest started.

He subsisted on apples juice, candies, coconut juice, and a bit of Jell-O. He wanted his stomach and intestines to be devoid of food, so he took laxatives to purge himself out and cleanse his innards. Of course, the unfortunate consequence of this was that he had to run to the restroom as fast as he could before soiling himself. In a nutshell, he ended up with a severe case of diarrhea.

It was a hotly contested competition between the chicken farm group and the young people from the orphanage. At the end of four rounds of battling, the score was tied at 7-7. As JT expected, the joust needed a tie-breaker. Having taken the necessary steps the night before to put him in a position to win, he easily bested these overmatched competitors. He was the runaway winner by a wide margin. He ate fifty-three eggs (move aside, Cool Hand Luke) in a ten-minute span. He was able to do that by mashing the egg yolk portions of ten boiled eggs, then added some water (each contestant was given two cups of water to aid in swallowing) to mix them into a slurry, finally drinking that semi-liquid mixture. Once he chewed down the cooked egg whites of the ten eggs, he repeated the procedure.

Dominic, the no-good, hot-tempered chicken farm bully, was able to stay close to this "Cooler Hand Young Luke" during the first minute of the competition, but faded quickly after that. The eventual runner-up, a pot-bellied behemoth of a farm worker, ate thirty-nine hard-boiled eggs.

To the victors went the spoils. Even though the awards were meager, the orphanage kids were celebrating like crazy. A lot of people didn't understand why, but for the young wards who had practically nothing, of having moments of helplessness, of questioning the very nature of their existence, of going through countless moments of sadness and despair, who never had anything to celebrate for, this was *their moment of triumph*. It not only provided a temporary escape from the harsh reality of their miserable lives, but it was an exhilarating feeling to finally had something positive to cheer about. So they celebrated like they won a hard-fought World Series, a bone-breaking Super Bowl battle or a triple overtime Game 7 of an instant classic NBA (National Basketball Association) championship. Some of the victorious kids even did victory laps around the chicken farm; several of them hoisted JT on their shoulders, chanting, "MVP (most valuable player)! MVP! MVP!"

One would think that the afternoon games of fun had ended with this picture-perfect conclusion.

But *rarely is the ending perfect*.

This excessive celebration drove Dominic the Bully into a tizzy, muttering and cursing in the most vile, foul words ever spoken in his native Tagalog dialect.

CHAPTER 27

THE BOUNCING EGG

After an afternoon filled with laughter, friendly teasing, boisterous fun, and joyous celebrations for the victorious orphanage group, it was time to help clean up the mess. It was accomplished in a very quick and efficient manner since everybody pitched in; they organized into five groups with distinct clean-up responsibilities.

Sister Pat sent word to remind the youngsters from the orphanage that a special motivational speaker would be coming at 6:00 p.m. that night. Most of this kids left soon afterward, needing to get washed up and rested before the night's program at the orphanage.

But Mark and JT decided to tarry a bit longer since Berto wanted to show them something. Berto is a great guy to have around. He loved fun, always bursting into minutes-long bouts of howls of laughter when he was told or retold a joke, even if the joke wasn't even that funny. He also shared an occasional tall tale or two. He had an interesting hobby, which was made possible because he was so willing do chores for Patrick, the farm supervisor.

It was an "I scratch your back, now you scratch my back, too" type of arrangement. Berto periodically got some undersized eggs that got rejected by the quality control people. These rejects normally got thrown into a big, blue, plastic-lined garbage can, later to be sold as animal feed.

But with Patrick's tacit approval, Berto would regularly get some of these discards.

So when the clowning Jake saw those rejects inside a bowl on the chicken farm boy's desk, he couldn't resist showing off his juggling skills. Initially, he was able to get six eggs in the air and was masterfully juggling them. But he lost his concentration when the mean-spirited Dominic appeared from nowhere. This bully was still pissed that the orphanage boys won the game, and Jake became the target of his intense wrath. He started approaching the still-juggling Jake while cursing profanely in his native tongue.

JT, distracted by Dominic's demeanor, lost his concentration, the consequence of which created a comedic scene. One of the undersized eggs fell and cracked on his head, so he was crowned with a broken yolk, and the slimy egg white dripped down his face.

Dominic was so pleased at the hilarious scene that he went away laughing his head off.

But what happened to one of the remaining eggs was quite mysterious. While the four eggs broke on different areas of the floor, the fifth one just bounced, bounced, bounced, and then rolled away. Curious, JT picked up the egg and cracked it open. To his and Mark's shock, the contents of the bouncing egg consisted only of solidified egg white. They couldn't figure out how the egg yolk became missing, and what caused the egg white to become denatured and turned solid.

CHAPTER 28

FREAKY CHICKS AND PULLETS

This particular layer farm didn't have a hatchery. But with the aid of Melchior (aka Mel), the veterinary student working part time in the farm, Berto was able to make the few of these rejected undersized eggs hatch. He was successful in patiently nurturing some of the little chicks into pullets, but because he wanted to raise these poultry cage-free, he let these fifteen-week-old hens roam the grounds of the farm.

It was a big mistake.

He suspected that some dishonest workers took the opportunity to turn those tender avians into a native delicacy called *adobong manok* (chicken cooked in soy sauce and vinegar).

Anita took pity when she saw Berto during one of his futile attempts to find his missing young hens. She confided to the poor teen that some-body had been going to the kitchen when the cafeteria was closed to "borrow" a deep fryer, returning it after a few days all dirtied, oily, and had a faint smell of fried chicken meat. This news made the usually jovial farm worker mad.

He said, "Bastards turned my pullets into KFC fried chicken!"

The only one that got spared was the two-headed hen, definitely because of the novelty of it. But Berto was anxious to show JT and Mark a couple of his two-week-old chicklets. Not wanting others to avail of free food ever again at his expense, he decided to raise his poultry in cages. Berto excitedly pointed out to his two friends, as he grabbed hold of a couple of the small chicks.

The one on his left hand was an adorable three-legged chick and his right hand cradled a tiny three-winged one. JT was especially dumb-struck, as he had taken a college course that taught statistics. Even though he got just a B for that course, he knew of the statistical improbability of finding three freaks of nature in one small chicken farm. He surmised that there is something weird happening. He postulated that something from the air, water, or soil was causing the mutations; the starter feeds were the culprit; some cosmic rays were emitting DNA (deoxyribonucleic acid)-altering beams on the farm; or some unknown radioactive source from nearby was causing all these weirdness.

He wasn't sure about the last hypothesis, since he had keenly observed that none of the workers had three legs, three arms, or two heads. He made a mental note to check with the barrio doctor, who did his rounds once a week, about the symptoms of radiation sickness or whether an increased cases of cancer-like episodes were being observed or complained about by workers in the chicken farm.

JT didn't know if it was one of Berto's tall tales, but this fatty young farm worker swore that he once raised a layer that had two anuses. He further recounted that it was hilarious to watch when eggs came out of the anuses in an alternating fashion. But the thing that might be more credible was the story about the workers hearing weird noises coming from the egg layer house closest to the back gate. These workers claimed that nocturnal creatures were doing crazy stuff in that henhouse late at night. A few who were brave enough to look inside could only see blurred images of unusually tall humanoids moving about and making rustling noises. It was such a weird, eerie, and hair-raising scary experience for the workers that they stopped going there to investigate.

This made sense to JT. It would explain the yolk-less egg. Somehow, these "aliens" were siphoning off the egg yolk, probably occurring in a way that the remaining egg white got denatured and turned into something rock-solid.

Mark nudged Jake toward the direction of the orphanage, reminding him of the program at 6:00 p.m. that night. But curiosity got the best of the soon-to-be college junior, so he told his friend Mark to go ahead, promising to follow in a little bit. Jake walked Mark to the front gate, nonchalantly waving as his orphanage friend faded into the distance.

CHAPTER 29

JT, the Hybrid Alien

Chapters 29 to 33 are dedicated to the memory of Eugene Wesley Roddenberry, sci-fi writer extraordinaire.

Gene,
You "live long and prosper!" You are always in the mind and soul of each and every die-hard Trekkie.

Jake went directly to the henhouse adjacent to the back gate. Karte, the security guard, saw him and motioned the college kid to come toward him. So JT grudgingly approached the sun-beaten man. After exchanging greetings, JT inquired about the old guard's knowledge of rumors of giant alien sightings inside the egg-layer house. The guard let out a laugh, stating assertively that those were just old wives' tales. Unconvinced, the handsome teenager went inside the henhouse to investigate. He found no alien, giant or otherwise.

He tried to search for clues by inspecting the newly laid eggs. But he didn't find too many, since most of them had already been collected by 4:00 p.m. The few that he was able to scrutinize looked and felt normal. So, he made a mental note to drop by this poultry house at a time much later in the night. He was convinced that whatever was transpiring and whatever strange things being done on some of the eggs occurred nocturnally. He made a decision to come back in the middle of the night this coming Saturday.

As he exited the red-painted layer house, he distinctly heard a plea: "Help... Help... Help me." He sensed that the sound came from the grove of mango trees that were about 160 meters from the back gate. But, he reasoned, that wasn't very possible, since he knew that the range of a human voice couldn't go that far. He ran toward Karte and asked the guard, "Did you hear that plea for help?"

The old man looked at him quizzically, then he retorted, "You stayed too long cooped up there, now the odious smell of all that chicken shit is making you hallucinate."

Jake started to believe the guard, that he was just imagining things, but as he started to walk away, he heard the plea for help again. So, he turned around and looked at the security guy, but the old man was going about his business; he didn't seem to hear anything, and his demeanor indicated that nothing was amiss.

Then it dawned on Jake. The plea for help was done not through sound but, rather, through thought. Someone or something was out there, definitely wounded and pleading for assistance through ESP (extrasensory perception). *Mental telepathy!* he thought.

The realization suddenly hit him: he possessed nonhuman qualities. He was able to destroy the elevator doors with a leg kick, he vomited gooey slime the color of rose gold, his blood had a shiny sheen, and now a freakish telepathic power!

Jake began to ask questions about himself and his parents. *Am I an alien from outer space? Am I a hybrid, a mixed alien? How did it happen? Is my mom the alien who I got these powers from? Is it my dad who is the alien? How come I look like a human? Who is my alien father? Or who is my alien mother? Am I an alien at birth? If not an alien at birth, at what stage of my life did I turn into an alien? So many questions, and no answer at all! Oh, it is so frustrating!*

Trying to answer the plea for help, he asked to borrow a first-aid kit from Karte. Holding the kit on his left hand, he opened the back gate with the other hand and hurriedly ran toward the source of the mental request for help. Even in his haste, he still saw that the two-headed chicken also sprinted out of the compound at the same instant he was coming out of the back gate. He wanted to keep going and take care of the poultry freak later (it had decided to enjoy a temporary freedom at the worst possible time), but he recalled Berto's heightened annoyance whenever one of his pet fowls went missing.

Jake felt that he had no other choice but to try to catch that mischievous avian, or at least shoo it back into the farm through the back gate. He got lucky, in the sense that he was successful in first his attempt to corral the freak and swiftly deposited it back to the compound.

After that, he went running at breakneck speed toward the mango trees. At this instance, he discovered another freakish power that he didn't know he had—he could run at an incredibly fast clip. He didn't measure the time it took to get to the spot a hundred meters away, but he felt certain that he easily bested Usain Bolt's world-record time by at least three seconds.

He was about seventeen meters from reaching the perceived location of the wounded alien being when he tripped over something. His tunnel-vision focus on a matter on hand occasionally led up to clumsy mishap such as this. He picked himself up and dusted himself off, and curiously investigated the offending item that caused his fall.

He found a 6.5 inch × 4.5 inch × 3.5 inch rectangular container. The material used to make that container wasn't familiar to him. It had a black, grainy surface, yet flexible, quite sturdy, and stretchable. It was puzzling, though, that the outsides of the container were so darn cold. But what really shocked him was the symbol adorning the top of the rectangular box: a *pink CROSS.*

The cross is a universal symbol of the risen Christ. Could this be the reason why the Second Coming of the Son of God seemed to be delayed for so long, to the dismay of some impatient, Earth-based Christians? That the grace of an Omniscient, Almighty Being is also being bestowed to other universes and to nonhuman aliens? That Jesus is tarrying too long because he needed to do some evangelizing elsewhere, too? That Jesus is also spreading the same message of salvation to alien-populated universes?

And yet, because of the uniform narrow-mindedness and close-heartedness of the residents of varying and wide-ranging universes, both human and alien, is the Gospel of Christ not only being rejected by an unbelieving Earth-based people but also by many other alien races? And that Jesus is constantly and repeatedly being crucified and rising on the third day in each of the heathen or unbelieving places He visited?

CHAPTER 30

THE ENCOUNTER

It suddenly registered on JT's mind that the plea for help came from a being not of this Earth, so he placed the first-aid kit inside a rattan basket lying nearby. He intended to pick it up on his way back, but for now, he didn't need that particular kit. He tucked the alien-aid kit he found underneath his left arm, but feeling the intense cold radiating from it through his skin, he decided it was best to carry it another way.

But curiosity got the best of him. He was wondering how the kit got to be so cold, with no evident electric connection or battery source or dry ice being present. He opened the kit, revealing fourteen slots for vials. But only seven vials were in that container. He lifted the vials one by one—all were almost frozen. Every one of those vials looked identical, except one that was missing a certain part compared to the others. He poked around for the cooling source or a battery or a miniature cooling machine of some sort, but found nothing. He marveled at the advanced alien technology.

Another thing he noticed was a neatly folded smaller version of this highly flexible, highly pliant container, tucked underneath the tray that held the vials. He closed the lid of the kit, wrapped his kerchief around it, and held it with his left hand. It was getting dark and the prevalent practice of Filipino mango growers made the job of finding the wounded alien a tougher chore.

·········

These growers believe that by putting a smoking source near the base of the mango trees, it allows the smoke to permeate the air, thereby inducing the trees to flower more. It is believed that this ancient practice yields a crop that is at least forty percent more than the usual harvest. It is postulated that it is the ethylene gas in the smoke that induces more flowering. Commercial growers in the USA do use ethylene gas, but for the purpose of accelerating the ripening process for green mangoes, green bananas, unripe tomatoes, etc.

·········

With all the tear-inducing smoke clouding the air, locating the alien was an impossibility. So, Jake took out his iPhone and used it as a flashlight to look around. Not finding the wounded alien, a question popped out of his mind, *Where the heck are you?*

To his utter amazement, his mind received a reply, saying, *Walk eighteen more steps toward the right.*

Jake took about ten steps to the right. Seeing or sensing nothing, he began doubt himself. Aloud, he muttered, "To *my* right or to *his* right?" But as he tiptoed a couple more steps forward, he could hear the moans of the wounded alien. He used that animalistic, eerie, blood-curling sound as a beacon to pinpoint the exact location of the possibly mortally-wounded creature.

When Jake reached the creature, he saw, silhouetted against the setting sun, a humanoid at least a foot taller than him. Next to the alien, he was a midget.

CHAPTER 31

THE ELIXIR

The alien giant was propped up against a pile of dried bamboo poles, breathing laboriously and in a semiconscious state. Even against the fading light, Jake could see the slow but steady flow of sparkly, viscous brown fluid oozing out of an open cut on its left arm. What concerned Jake the most was the gaping wound just below its right rib cage.

There was a circular hole may be two to three inches in diameter, just a bit above and to the right of the navel, where the alien's fluids was spurting out. JT removed the kerchief that was acting as his insulation against the ice-cold surface of the alien "first-aid" kit. He then neatly folded it and pressed the cloth on top of the wound, hoping to stop any further loss of alien blood.

The coldness of the kerchief produced an instant but incongruous reaction: the expected reflexive jerking avoidance or withdrawing movement from something really cold versus the soothing effect of the cold cloth pressed on a still-bleeding, very raw wound. The application of this cold compress caused the wounded alien to stir up and move about, and JT could see the enormous effort being exerted by the alien to try to become fully conscious.

Encouraged, the UCSD student opened up the small cartoon of

coconut juice that he was carrying and forced some of the liquid down the slight opening at the edge of the alien's mouth.

It was an asinine move.

The alien's reaction was part comedic and part frightening. The first movement was akin to that of burning charcoal being rammed down a person's pants. The frightening part was the alien's allergic reaction to the foreign liquid—red rashes, itchy hives, and nasty boils breaking out, as well as sneezing, wheezing, shortness of breath, coughing, and vomiting.

The extraterrestrial spat out the coco water and mentally telegraphed JT an inquiring question. *Are you trying to kill me?*

Jake was mortified. He apologized profusely for his ignorance. At that point, he noticed another anatomical difference in this alien. There was an orifice atop the left shoulder that opened up whenever there was a sudden need for a quick supply of oxygen. He observed the hole opening up when the giant visitor from outer space was experiencing shortness of breath and was gasping for air.

The only positive that came out of his unintentional food poisoning of the giant was that it catapulted this gentle humanoid back to the realm of full consciousness. Now fully aware of the severity of his wounds, the space traveler instructed the helpful teen to hand him one of the seven vials.

Jake estimated that each vial contained about 10 ml. The wounded alien first warmed the cold vial by holding it tight in his left hand for a few seconds, then turned over the vial so that the bottom of the container was up. He opened the tiny hidden lid at the bottom of the vial, pouring its 6 ml contents on the wounds on his left arm and stomach. The action of this healing liquid on the wounds was miraculous. There was this fizzling, bubbling, and cauterizing effect, followed by an incredible, instantaneous healing of the wounds. But what happened next is nothing short of magic.

This 6 ml of wound-healing solution was, in reality, contained in the outer chamber of the vial. But look hard and inspect carefully, and one would find—hidden in an opaque, nearly indiscernible inner chamber—the other 4 ml of the wonder drug, the miracle elixir.

The alien flipped or pressed something on the top end of the vial, and out flowed 4 mℓ of the precious elixir—which were previously hidden in the inner chamber—into his open, waiting mouth. The magical effect is instantaneous.

The alien seemed so alive and strong again. A complete, instantaneous rejuvenation, and any visible signs of either arm or stomach wounds were erased. JT thought, *I will definitely ask the dude for a free sample.*

CHAPTER 32

THE GIFT

Once the giant alien was able to catch his breath and got rested, he thanked the young man immensely. He told JT that the six remaining vials were his gift to him, tokens of his appreciation for saving his life.

The visitor from outer space also told him that the subzero temperatures inside the container will maintain the potency of the elixirs for many years. Once any vial was taken out of the cold kit, however, the effectiveness of the liquid elixir inside that particular vial loses its potency unless refrozen within four hours or cryogenically stored. The alien also mentioned that there was a smaller folded case under the tray of vials that could also keep these elixirs at subzero temperatures.

Jake was curious as to why there was one vial that had no inner chamber, so the alien told him that he carried that particular vial in case of possible "life or death" situations. Better to give up a vial full of cleansing/healing solution rather than give up a vial that had 4 mℓ of the miracle rejuvenating solution.

The alien also confided to JT that since these elixirs were made by alien scientists, the healing and rejuvenating effects were not as instantaneous or dramatic as what the youngster witnessed as compared when used for humans. The healing effects needed a longer time to kick in; the rejuvenating effect took longer to become effective; and its effect might, in some cases, be temporary.

But there were also two other very important differences when these alien-manufactured medicines were used by humans. Even the alien scientists working on these miracle drugs were amazed and impressed by their findings. They found out about the incredible effects when these were used on some of the human guinea pigs.

(Note: much of Book Two of the six-part series will focus on the stupefying results of this wonder drug on humans—and all the good and bad things that might result as a consequence of the relative availability of these elixirs.)

Jake was curious why the egg yolk was being drained off from the eggs. The alien mentally replied, *Patience, little grasshopper. That will all be revealed in due time.*

(Note: that mystery will be explained in Book Three.)

The gentle alien asked JT to accompany him to an area roughly halfway between the henhouse and the mango grove. Once they arrived there, the alien gave Jake a device that would alert this *Amboy* that the giant humanoid was back on Earth, and would also allow JT to contact the alien. After a tight farewell embrace, a gateway magically appeared. The outer space giant entered the portal and disappeared into another universe.

Just when the college kid was feeling good about his heroics, out of the shadows, the mean-spirited Dominic the bully, with his iPhone video still recording, emerged.

CHAPTER 33

BAD NEWS REVEALED

Dominic told JT that he had recorded the miraculous recovery of the alien on his knock-off iPhone. He tried to intimidate Jake into turning over the vials, promising a severe beating should the college kid refused. But this super boy knew now that he possessed a devastatingly powerful kick, and also a newly discovered ability to outrun anybody. Besides, JT was a full four inches taller than the bully. Even though the chicken-farm worker had a very taut, lean, and ripped body due to the hard labor of his chores (which he abhorred doing but had no choice) at the farm, Jake felt he had the necessary survival skills to defend himself against this menacing adversary.

But his dad taught JT to be a pacifist at all costs. "Never engage in any physical fisticuffs," Jerry used to advise his son. "Rather, use your creative mind to wiggle out of any spot."

So the unnaturally gifted JT put his amazing speed on display. He shifted to hyperdrive, orphanage-bound, without breaking any sweat. Just as he passed the farm bully, he yelled, "Eat my dust! Catch me if you can!"

He arrived at the orphanage at around 6:45 p.m. He muttered, "Dang! How time really flies!" He tiptoed past the room where the speaker was giving his speech about positive thinking, barely glancing at the faces of the captivated, eager audience.

Holding the super-cold alien kit like it was a hot potato, he hastily went to his room. Once there, he opened the kit, lifted the tray, took out the smaller container that was neatly folded under the tray, and molded it into its intended shape. It formed a rectangular box (similar to a cigar box) that had space for six vials. He held his right hand just above the box, trying to feel if it was giving the needed subzero temperature. Satisfied, he transferred five of the vials, leaving the "decoy" vial in the larger kit.

He intended to hide the smaller kit containing the precious elixirs at the bottom of his traveling bag, but in the process of doing so, he came across the unopened letter from his mom. A rush of emotion filled him.

He knew that the letter contained bad news, the severity of which he didn't know. He promised his mom that he wouldn't open the letter until three weeks of JT's semestral break had elapsed, and today was only day eighteen. But he got the elixir needed to potentially cure his mom of whatever sickness she might have.

Conflicted, but elated at the prospect of having a miracle cure, he opened the letter. He was still floored by the gravity of the bad news: Mary had stage four breast cancer, and was told that she had, at most, two months left to live. He was quite saddened and distraught, unwilling to accept the cruel fate that befell his mom.

He then made a resolute decision to catch the next plane back to California as soon as possible.

CHAPTER 34

UTTER CRAZINESS

Jake did not bother to listen to what the farm bully was trying to say, for he knew that this mean-spirited dude would want to use this opportunity to grab his fifteen minutes of fame. Dominic was talking excitedly in Tagalog, arms gesticulating and flailing. Then the TV (television) played the poor and grainy video that the bad dude recorded.

Jake was thankful that the lighting on the video was dim, it being recorded during twilight. Both JT's and the gentle alien's faces were barely discernible. All that could be inferred from the three-and-a-half minute of recording was a giant of a being that seemed mortally wounded; a vial of something that did what appeared to be a miraculous thing, magically transforming what seemed to be a near-dead humanoid into one who was super alive and alert; and that the giant looked to have disappeared into a weird portal.

This news event sparked a frenzy like no other. Most of the news for the following days suddenly focused on UFO (unidentified flying object) sightings, alien abductions, alleged presence of aliens among humans, cloaking technology that allowed aliens to hide their presence, superior alien technology that let them alter humans' perception of extraterrestrials' physical features, human women being used as breeders for Earth-alien half-breeds, and Earth Valentinos and Lotharios being enslaved as boy toys of sex-crazed alien amazons.

Some celebrities and business leaders who were alleged to be outer-space entities:

- Harvey Weinstein was alleged to have acquired a physically-altered Earthling appearance, but was an abused and maltreated alien from a faraway galaxy where he came from
- Kevin Spacey
- Bill Cosby
- Tom Brokaw
- Matt Lauer
- Charlie Rose

Hilarious and weird books started coming out in prints, too, with titles like:

My Alien Lover
My Uncle the Martian
The Insatiable Alien
My Aunt the Venusian
Diary of an Extra-Terrestrial
Alien Abduction: Part 9
Intimate Encounter for the Fifth Time
My 2 Alien Lotharios: The Dashing Mexican and the Energizer Bunny Plutonian

Not to be outdone, the snake oil salesmen came out in droves. Useless concoctions and ineffective liquids were being sold as the real McCoy.

All these craziness might just be more than enough reasons for the aliens who were probably already living among humans to scare them off and prompt them to take an extended vacation in their alien homeland.

Even the egg-layer poultry farm wasn't spared. It got turned into a novelty site: an amusement park!

Admission fees were charged for entry to the henhouses. Seven scheduled daily tours of the farm always got sold out. A dollar fee was charged for taking photos with alien-costumed characters. Berto made it, minting oodles of money by charging for the privilege of showing his freaky chicks.

What a BIZZARRO world!

But the big bad dude Dominic wasn't only going after his fifteen minutes of fame. He craved to be rich, too. He knew he couldn't force Jake to hand over the vials of elixir on his own, so he enlisted the assistance of the meanest and most ruthless of them all, the infamous Kumander Karding.

CHAPTER 35

THE SWAP

Kumander Karding started as an ideologue and practitioner of Communism. He and his fellow communists would rob the rich plantation owners and distribute the loot to the poor. But as they became known and feared by the community, they started to impose "revolutionary taxes" on the well-heeled as well as the poor.

This ill-advised move diminished whatever good will they had initially built. Their reputation as modern-day Robin Hoods suffered even more when the group started committing abuses and atrocities.

Seeing the success of other bandit groups that were now engaged in new criminal enterprises, Karding, the chief *bandido*, decided that his group might as well reap the rewards of those devious schemes, too. His group initially picked on the easy targets: middle-class travelers and the plain, old hardworking businessmen. It was easy pickings, like stealing candy from a baby. Just by threatening to extinguish their comfortable lives, those poor souls got so scared that they willingly forked over what they had in their wallets or in their possession.

But the mean "Bandit King of the South" wanted more action, and decided to go big time. So he resorted to kidnapping the wealthy merchants. He is now playing in the BIG leagues, and this type of criminal activity could be hazardous to the health of both him and his men.

In the big leagues, the rules of the game are different. First, the rich are high profile and semi-celebrities, so any bit of news, whether good or bad, would definitely be an item on the news broadcast. Second, these are well-moneyed folks, which mean they could afford the services of highly trained, very skilled, and heavily armed bodyguards. As a consequence, the specter of heavy fighting and possibility of debilitating injuries or casualties between two equally armed groups were not to be discounted. Third, these elite, powerful, and ultra-rich folks had cultivated great relationships with top generals of the armed forces and police chiefs nationwide, so it is easy to request assistance or reinforcements from governmental forces at any time.

Despite all these factors, Kumander Karding had some success as the head of this kidnap-for-ransom group. Oh, they did lose some members in a couple of intense firefights, but they were also able to score big in three or four highly lucrative operations. With the lion's share of those ransom money, the chief bandit, by all measures of wealth, is now considered a rich man. He is now at the stage of contemplating retirement, hoping to finally enjoy the ill-gotten spoils by buying a gigantic hacienda or several coconut plantations.

But he needed to make one more big score, one that would catapult him into becoming a newly-minted multimillionaire.

So when the chicken farm bully approached Kumander Karding with a kidnapping proposal that could potentially yield millions of dollars, he was a willing and eager listener.

Dominic presented a simple plan: kidnap one of Jake's relatives and exchange that hostage for one or more of those magical elixirs. Since the footage documenting the miracle curing effectiveness of the elixir was shown throughout the whole world, it is a cinch that both of them could reap tens of millions of dollars for each of those elixirs in a highest-bidder type of auction.

The crime boss liked the simplicity of the plan. He marveled at how a simpleton of a farm worker could concoct a harebrained scheme that might actually work.

They figured JT's maternal Uncle Reggie is the college student's favorite Philippine-based relative, so they focused on using him as a kidnapping target. The added bonus is that they are familiar with the copra trader, since some of Karding's men had already participated in robbing Reggie once.

It wasn't an extremely difficult task, but it came with casualties on both sides. Both Reggie's bodyguards were killed, but the group lost two members as well.

Dominic the bully then began the negotiations with Jake. The *Amboy* showed more resolve and maturity than they expected. At first, JT refused the idea of an Uncle Reggie-for-elixir swap, even showing the temerity to threaten them by promising to report their kidnapping scheme to the authorities. But when Dominic threatened to have Reggie executed via decapitation, the youngster from Glendale, California relented.

Jake was adamant, however, on his condition that only one vial would be traded in exchange for Reggie's life. Dominic the bully wasn't willing to budge, since he wanted at least two of those wonder drug-elixirs. But his instincts told him to consult with Kumander Karding. The evil boss knew he would still be able to get tons of money for that lone precious vial, so he OK'd the deal.

JT was forced to exchange a vial for the life of his favorite uncle. After the exchange was made, both nephew and badly-tortured uncle were covertly transported to Manila, the ancient capital of the Philippines. It was done using the cover of darkness and under heavy military escort.

On the road to Manila, Jake was telepathically thanking the gentle alien for having the prescience to have an elixir-less vial ready for a situation such as this.

CHAPTER 36

ELIXIR FOR MOMMY DEAREST

Jake wasted no time. He asked his dear Uncle Reggie to accompany him to the Ninoy Aquino International Airport. His uncle reluctantly agreed to drop off the anxious youngster for his return flight to the USA. Both uncle and nephew hugged tightly, with the young man planting a tender kiss on the left cheek of his dear relative. They said their cursory good-byes, then JT went straight to the departure lounge, awaiting the boarding call for the Los Angeles-bound PAL (Philippine Airlines) flight.

While waiting patiently to board, he received a sweet text message from his dear Julie, which read, *"Au revoir and bon voyage! Good-bye is not forever. See you soon!"*

He was a bit puzzled with the last part of the message. Was it in the literal or figurative sense? Did the object of his affection, the always-thoughtful and loving Julie, had travel plans that he wasn't aware of? Hopeful of such a possibility, it made his heart skip a beat or two.

The young man was able to catch the last flight of the day. He couldn't help but be excited about the prospect of having the miracle cure for his dying mom right there in his carry-on bag. Upon his arrival at the Los Angeles International Airport some twelve hours later, he immediately hopped inside an Uber for the forty-minute trip to his mom's condo. Not finding her there, he texted her, but there was no response. So he texted one of her US-based sisters.

His aunt responded, *"She is confined at Kaiser Sunset, she is quite weak, undergoing radiation and chemotherapy combo treatment."*

Jake hurriedly went down to the underground garage where he left his Toyota Camry some twenty-one days ago and drove his car impatiently to the Kaiser hospital at Los Angeles. Arriving there, he broke into a sprint after leaving the car with the valet, and quickly reached the receptionist's area. He requested a visitor's tag and got his mom's room number from the friendly receptionist. He didn't even consider using the elevator, deciding on using his hyper-speed instead to get to his mom's room.

Finding the room, JT knocked softly and then let himself in. His mom was sedated and seemed to be trying her best to get out of her induced dreamy state, in her attempt to acknowledge the presence at the door. He rushed to her side, gently and tenderly caressing her back. He was quite shocked at the complete change of her appearance from several weeks ago. She lost a lot of weight and clumps of her hair had fallen off. JT was on the verge of tears when he saw his dear mom in such a sorry, pitiful state. There were several IV tubes attached to both her arms, and a breathing tube was dangling, too, all the way to her chest. Worse, needles punctured her hands, and there were terrible, deep-purple bruises evident on both of them.

He found himself being eyed and gazed upon intently by his still-groggy mom. When their eyes locked, the gravity of her situation and the realization that his mom was definitely at the terminal phase of her life caused both to burst into tears. The ever-loving son rushed to give Mary a tender embrace, careful to navigate his way around the dangling web of IV tubes. Mother and son were locked in this tight and loving embrace.

With tears now flowing free from his handsome face, Jake excitedly narrated the fortuitous events that led up to his possession of the miracle elixir. Mary was somewhat skeptical, yet, at the same, welcomed the possibility that opened a way for her to get out of her life-ending situation. The now-rapidly maturing son opened the lid of the outer chamber of the vial and poured the liquid on the outer surface of his mom's hands, where there were many needle puncture marks. Having accomplished that, he then poured the miracle cure, that precious elixir, into his mom's now open mouth. Then he allowed his exhausted mother to slip back to her dreamy, sedated state. He then sat on a chair at the foot of her bed and waited.

CHAPTER 37

WHERE ART THY STING?

"Where, O death, is thy victory?"

1 CORINTHIANS 15:55 (WNT [WEYMOUTH NEW TESTAMENT])

M ary slowly but surely recovered from her near brush with death. After two months, her oncologists were astounded at her cancer-free status. Not only was her disease in total remission, all the symptoms associated with this deadly malady were now gone. The doctors attributed this miracle to either being a loving act of God or through Mary's prayerful ways. One thing was certain, though, the evidence was indisputable.

Jake's mom was now slowly gaining her weight and strength back. The doctors mentioned that she should be able to be back to work in ten days' time. Mother and son spent the last three weeks of JT's semestral break, which Jake was supposed to spend in the orphanage, bonding and basking in familial warmth. Although he periodically lamented the abrupt termination of the latter half of his supposed six-week stay at the orphanage, all in all, he was happy about the eventual turn of events. The only regret he had was the missed opportunity to develop something special with Julie. He used the last three weeks of his summer break to care for and help nurse his mom back to health.

But the three weeks went by so fast. It was now mid-September, and so with a sad and heavy heart, he reluctantly left his mom and moved back to San Diego. A brand-new school year beckoned, ushering him to the start of his junior year in college.

....

Needing to do a bit of math, Jake tried to account for all the seven vials of the elixirs that he found in that alien kit. One vial was used by the alien behemoth. The elixir-free vial was used to buy Uncle Reggie's freedom. Another vial of elixir was used to save her mom from stage four cancer. So that still left him with four vials.

He was now inundated with pleas for the wonder drug, thanks but no thanks to that farm bully Dominic. Generous offers of cash, houses, cars, limited-mintage gold coins, diamonds, rare stamps collections, and such were proposed as barter for these miracle potions. He was embarrassed when he was bombarded with several propositions of marriage in exchange for the much-in-demand wonder medical elixirs.

Jake knew there was only one person he could turn to, somebody who could make the most logical and smart decision regarding the fate of these four vials of elixirs—his dad.

Jerry was quite elated about the wonderful miracle that the elixir did for Mary. He had stayed with his ex-love at the Kaiser hospital for three days prior to Jake's arrival from Asia. The ex-professor was despondent when the doctors told him that his former partner would physically cease to exist, generously speaking, in about a month's time. That the elixir was able to reverse the ravages of the disease and allow Mary to escape the near-terminal grip of the deadly stage four cancer was simply mind-boggling, awe-inspiring, and providential.

Being rooted firmly in his Christian faith and values, Jerry felt, deep in his heart, that the miraculous recovery of Mary was a heaven-orchestrated assist. It was only through the compassionate and tender, loving care of the Almighty that such a blessing and a glorious miracle occurred.

Not wanting to waste a grand opportunity to use these vials of magical elixirs to benefit a swath of humanity, Jerry and his young son JT came out with this bold, exceedingly-brilliant move: they would auction off, to the highest bidders, two of the four vials of miracle potions.

CHAPTER 38

THE GRAND VISION

Father and son decided to take the following course of action: One vial would stay with Jake for safekeeping. Another vial would be shipped to this G-14 government researcher, with the elixir inside cryogenically frozen. Jerry would perform studies and thorough, exhaustive investigations to identify the possible source or origins of its miracle-performing properties. Two vials would be auctioned off to separate individuals in a highest-bidder format. In addition, there were also stipulations that the winning bidders must agree to.

These two winning bidders must be financially capable and are good global citizens. They must each do an annual cumulative 500 hours of service to benefit the needy, the poor, and the unfortunate. In addition to their winning bids, each one of these successful bidders must make annual donations of $10 million dollars for seven continuous years to a nonprofit charity fund that would be set up. This fund would be established with the sole purpose of helping the homeless, the destitute, the forgotten, and the forsaken of their community.

The *brilliance* of the plan is in the singularity of its purpose. Its sole purpose is to use the fund generated from the auction to benefit all of humanity. This is just a prototype, a scaled-down version of the grand vision that was inspired and revealed to the sagacious Jerry.

Because of the limitations presented by the availability of just two vials of the miracle drug, a much grander and more magnificent version would have to wait.

(Note: Book Two will solve the limited-availability problem of the magical elixir and will unfold the execution of the gloriously magnificent blueprint that the Almighty has planned to serve the poverty-stricken, hopeless, forsaken, and shunned segment of humanity.)

In this scaled-down prototype, all the homeless, the poor, the desperate, the neglected, the needy, and the destitute of El Monte and Baldwin Park, California, would be gathered and housed into a sparkling, newly built multipurpose ten-story building.

There would be an initial sorting out of this sad, miserable, and piteous group. The drug addicts and drug-dependents would be sent to rehab centers to wean them out of their addiction, and also to detoxify them. The alcoholics would be sent to proper institutions to eradicate their alcohol dependency. Those suffering from mental illness would be sent to institutions and psychiatric wards to give them the help they needed.

Once this sorting process was accomplished, then the difficult but necessary steps would follow. The building would serve not only as a shelter for these neglected, desperate, and shunned segment of society but also as a source of food for the physical body and provider of nourishment for the soul. In other words, the homeless shelter would provide nutritious meals for them. Then a rotating group of religious teachers and scholars would encourage and stimulate their spiritual growth.

But it is more than just a shelter. It is also to serve as a training and retraining center. These wretched group will be taught employable trades and skills, and eventually helped in securing jobs necessary to support their daily living. Once they are back on their feet and regained their self-worth, their self-confidence, and their sense of dignity, they will again be allowed to join the fold of society. They will become important contributors to a vibrant, thriving California economy. And the fervent hope is that, with their exposure to the teachings of religious scholars and educators, each one of them will now lead a life in harmony of God's grandiose plan for all of humanity.

·········

It is the simplicity of His design that is both awe-inspiring and glorious:

Each one of us exists in this physical world so that everyone is able to help, to care, and to love one another—in our own small way, to help make this world a warm, compassionate, loving, and better place (than before each one came into being). All these blessings—undeserved assistance and unearned grace freely bestowed by the Almighty—will hopefully encourage each one of us to live a life worthy of living, in a spirit of peace, care, harmony, and love.

·········

The auction came and went. The two winning bidders paid sixty-eight million dollars each for the privilege of owning one vial of the precious miracle elixir.

End

Book Two is entitled *Mystery of the Elixir – Solved*

References

"Just the Way You Are" by Bruno Mars

"Why Does Your Skin Age?" Dartmouth Undergraduate Journal of Science, 2013

"Overseas Chinese, Coolie, Guano Trade, Chinese Emigration." Wikipedia

"Elegance Presentation: Bouquet from Flower Direct." Ie

"Ready to Take a Chance again" by Barry Manilow

"Can't Smile Without You" by Barry Manilow

"Libido and Sigmund Freud." Wikipedia

"Libido Jungian Dream Analysis." FrithLuton.com

"Morning Sickness." Wikipedia, medicine plus.gov, americanpregnancy.org, medicalnewstoday.com, babycenter.com

"Pregnancy Kit." Wikipedia, todaysparent.com, healthline.com, fristresponse.com, parents.com bellybelly.com, emedicinehealth.com, healthline.com, webmd.com, wikihow.com, priyaring.com, the bump.com

"Layer Poultry Farm." growelagrovet.com, roysfarm.com, sildeshare.net, Wikipedia, scribd.com, agriframing.inagrihaelthfood.com

Ward, Phillip. *The Book of Common Fallacies: Falsehoods, Misconceptions, Flawed Facts, and Half-Truths That Are Ruining Your Life.*

Hudson, Irene. *Food Fads and Fallacies.*

"Brown Eggs Fallacies," the poultry monthly, Wikipedia, mentalfolls. com.

"Strangers in the Night" by Frank Sinatra

"Two Less Lonely People in the World" by Air Supply

"When I need You" by Leo Sayer

"Run for the Roses" by Dan Fogelberg

Schwantes, Carlos Arnaldo. *The Pacific Northwest: An Interpretive History.* Nebraska: University of Nebraska Press, 1996.

"American Merchants and the Chinese Coolie Trade 1850-1880: Contrasting Models of Human Trafficking to Peru and the United States." Austin Schultz, https://digitalcommons.wou.edu/his/7/

"Rugby Boys," en.m.wikipedia.org

Carlos Arnaldo Schwantes "The Pacific Northwest: An Interpretive History", University of Nebraska Press

Austin Schultz "American Merchants and the Chinese Coolie Trade 1850-1880", Digital commons@WOU

CPSIA information can be obtained
at www.ICGtesting.com
Printed in the USA
LVHW08*2149140918
590115LV00003B/4/P

9 781595 557698